When he sat next ... chaise, Damien c... than necessary, so that their thigh... rubbed against each other. It was a test of sorts, to see if he'd read her vibe correctly, or if he was completely off base.

He wasn't.

Instead of moving away, April leaned against him as she sipped her wine.

"Is this why you're okay not playing with an orchestra?" Damien asked her. "You can get your fix here?"

She shrugged. "I never thought about it that way, but I guess you're right. I miss the live shows, but I don't miss the hassle. Traveling from city to city takes its toll on you."

"You look no worse for the wear," he said, allowing his eyes to travel the length of her. His mouth watered at the sight of the smooth expanse of thigh peeking through the rip in her jeans.

When his eyes met hers again he noticed the subtle heat staring back at him. Damien traced her bare arm with the backs of his fingers, the caress hovering somewhere between a friendly stroke and something...more.

"Do you ever think about going back out there? Joining another orchestra?"

April's eyes slid closed. Damien wanted to think it was so she could concentrate on his touch. She took a sip of wine before answering.

Dear Reader,

For years I've written books set in my cherished home of south Louisiana, but I've shied away from even mentioning the storm that devastated the Gulf South back in 2005. This time, I decided to confront Hurricane Katrina head-on by setting *Passion's Song* in New Orleans's Ninth Ward neighborhood. I wanted to show both the struggles the area is still experiencing and the true courage that many of its residents have displayed as they continue to recover from Katrina's devastation.

Passion's Song is a story of strength, resilience and, of course, love. I hope you enjoy April and Damien's love story. I also hope that it gives you greater insight into the issues that remain a part of everyday life for many in my beloved New Orleans.

Farrah Rochon

PASSION'S
Song

Farrah Rochon

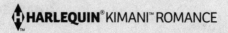

HARLEQUIN® KIMANI™ ROMANCE

Recycling programs
for this product may
not exist in your area.

ISBN-13: 978-0-373-86437-9

Passion's Song

Printed in U.S.A.

Farrah Rochon had dreams of becoming a fashion designer as a teenager, until she discovered she would be expected to wear something other than jeans to work every day. Thankfully, the coffee shop where she writes does not have a dress code. When Farrah is not penning stories, the *USA TODAY* bestselling author and avid sports fan feeds her addiction to football by attending New Orleans Saints games.

Books by Farrah Rochon

Harlequin Kimani Romance

Huddle with Me Tonight

I'll Catch You

Field of Pleasure

Pleasure Rush

A Forever Kind of Love

Always and Forever

Delectable Desire

Runaway Attraction

Yours Forever

Forever's Promise

A Mistletoe Affair

Forever with You

Stay with Me Forever

Passion's Song

Visit the Author Profile page at Harlequin.com for more titles.

Dedicated to my fellow Louisiana residents who are still bravely recovering from Hurricane Katrina.

But those who hope in the Lord will renew their strength. They will soar on wings like eagles; they will run and not grow weary, they will walk and not be faint.
—*Isaiah* 40:31

Acknowledgments

I'd like to thank Gravier Street Social in downtown New Orleans, local cellist Monica McIntyre and fellow writer Tiffany Monique. All influenced this story in their own special way.

Chapter 1

"Tonight calls for wine."

As April Knight surveyed the array of steno pads, highlighters and sticky notes strewn about her living room floor, she had to fight the urge to race to her bedroom and bury her head beneath the covers. There was so much work to do.

"Lots of wine," she said with a sigh.

Simeon Wilks, who dedicated much of his free time to volunteering with her at A Fresh Start, the teen summer program where she worked in New Orleans's Lower Ninth Ward, looked up from where he sat on the floor, his back against the sofa.

"I'm not so sure alcohol is the smartest idea," Simeon said. He tossed the documents he'd been skimming onto his lap. "But what the hell do I know? Bring me a beer."

"I'll take a glass of wine and I don't even drink," the program's director, LaDonna Miller, said.

"I'll be right back," April told them. "The pizza should be here any minute."

As if on cue, the doorbell rang.

"I'll take care of the pizza," Simeon said, rising from the floor with catlike agility and proving April just in her envy of the under-thirty crowd. She'd actually heard her thirty-five-year-old knees creak when she'd gotten out of bed that morning.

She stepped into the kitchen of the double shotgun house she'd bought when she returned to New Orleans two years ago. It was on the small side, but exactly the right size for her. Despite her urge to pull every bottle from the wine rack, April settled on a single bottle of pinot noir. Tonight was about coming up with solutions, not acquiring hangovers. They all needed to keep clear heads.

She slid two wine stems from the under-the-counter rack, grabbed a bottle of Abita lager from the fridge and lifted extra napkins from the stack she kept on the counter. Just as she started to make her way back to the living room, her phone vibrated in her pocket, signaling an incoming text.

She quickly unloaded the burden from her arms so she could check her phone. She'd been expecting to hear from her agent regarding a payment dispute with the production company she'd worked with back in March.

After traveling the globe for the past ten years as a concert cellist, April had decided she was done with being on the road. She'd found a way to earn a living while still indulging her love of music. Staying in one place had taken some adjustment, but April enjoyed the work she did now, providing music—usually remotely—for movies and television. This current dispute was for a concerto she'd provided for a luxury car brand's commercial.

However, the text she found when she pulled her phone from her pocket wasn't from Carlos Munoz, her agent. It was from Damien Alexander.

April's heart did a rodeo-style gallop within her chest.

Because her heart was a sappy dreamer that ignored insignificant things such as reality.

Damien's text was simple: Hi. Need to speak with you. Can we meet tomorrow?

April texted back: Hi, stranger. Sure. Meet me at AFS. Building across from Saint Katherine's Church.

His reply came seconds later. Thanks. Be there at 11 a.m.

April stared at the phone for several long, agonizing moments as she tried to decide if she should reply with a simple *thanks* or *see you then*. Would it make her look too eager? Would he think it was rude if she didn't reply at all?

"Oh, for crying out loud," April said under her breath.

She shoved the phone back into her pocket and picked up the things she'd set on the counter. Then she made her way back into her living room, where her colleagues were gathered.

Nicole Russell, who taught dance at A Fresh Start, sat on the floor next to Simeon.

"Hey, when did you get here?" April asked. "I thought you had a gig somewhere in Mandeville?"

"I came in with the pizza. My gig was canceled," Nicole said.

"Aw, I'm sorry," April said. "I know you were looking forward to it. Let me get another wineglass."

Nicole held up a soda bottle. "Thanks, but I'm good."

April placed the wine bottle and glasses next to the pizza box that lay open on the ash oak coffee table she'd picked up at a yard sale. After distributing the drinks, she picked up her slice of pizza and nodded to the white-board she'd propped against the back of the chair she'd brought in from the kitchen.

"Okay, let's hear it," April said. "How do we save A Fresh Start?"

"A Fresh Start doesn't need to be saved, does it?" Nicole asked. "The program is still in good shape."

"If it were in such good shape, we wouldn't be here tonight," LaDonna pointed out. Their director had called for tonight's meeting following their first week of operation for this summer's program. A Fresh Start might not have been in danger of closing as it had been in years past, but the program was definitely in need of help.

"We lost more than two dozen kids from last year," April said. "It would be one thing if we'd lost them to other summer programs, but Simeon went on a fact-finding mission yesterday and discovered that's not the case. Right?" April asked him.

He nodded. "Most of them were just hanging out at home, or around the neighborhood."

"Why didn't you grab them and make them come back to the center?" Nicole asked.

"Because that would be kidnapping," Simeon said around a mouthful of pepperoni.

"We can't force kids to attend A Fresh Start," April said. "Nor can we make their parents bring them. But we all know the more we keep them occupied and off the streets this summer, the better chance those kids have of staying out of trouble. We have to do something about this retention problem. We can't keep losing kids during the school year."

"I think we all know what the best solution is for keeping kids throughout the school year," LaDonna said with a resigned sigh.

Yes, they all knew. The problem was that expanding A Fresh Start into a year-round program would require more resources than they had at their disposal.

They were lucky enough to have volunteers who viewed the youth program as an essential part of their lives and not just a feel-good hobby they could drop without a moment's notice. They were a small group, but they were dedicated. However, manpower was only one part of the equation.

"Haven't we beaten this dead horse enough already?" Simeon said. "We all know that turning A Fresh Start into a year-round program instead of just a summer program would solve much of this problem, but that calls for money. Something we don't have."

He was right, and they all knew it. Keeping A Fresh Start open for at least two to three hours in the afternoon, during those hours between when kids were let out of school and when their parents arrived home from work, was a critical component to retaining the kids they'd managed to keep from last summer.

The program, which currently helped more than fifty children from around the neighborhood, relied on donations and creative budgeting to get by. But their anemic bank account barely had enough funds to cover their expenses for the next ten weeks. Stretching that to cover an entire year of programming?

"We have to figure out a way to make this happen,"

April said, her voice solemn. "Last summer Demarco Jackson was one of my most promising violinists. I was concerned when I didn't see him during our first week back. I found out from one of his schoolmates today that Demarco was picked up for truancy four times during the school year, and just got out of juvenile detention for a street fight he was involved in. Thankfully, it didn't turn more violent than a fistfight, but it could have gotten out of hand and led to something much more deadly."

April looked into the faces of each of her colleagues.

"I refuse to lose any of these kids to the streets," she continued with renewed determination. "We have something good going here. We need to make sure it continues to thrive."

"You're preaching to the choir," Nicole said. "We all know the benefit A Fresh Start brings to the Ninth Ward. But that doesn't solve the money problem."

"That's why we're here this evening, right?" April said. "We need to figure out how to come up with the funding we need."

She took a healthy sip from her wineglass, then slid off the sofa and walked over to the whiteboard. Uncapping a dry-erase marker, she scrawled *FUND-RAISING* across the top and turned to her colleagues.

"Okay," April said. "Let me have it."

Her request was met with blank expressions and deafening silence.

April tipped her head back and sighed at the ceiling. "Come on, you guys," she said. "This cannot be that hard. Just throw out some ideas."

She wrote *bake sale* on the whiteboard.

"Really?" came Nicole's laconic drawl. "You think

selling cakes and cookies is going to give us the kind of money we need to turn A Fresh Start into a year-round program?"

"No," April said. "But this is how you brainstorm. Start with the most obvious and just throw things out there until something sticks."

"The most obvious is acquiring more benefactors," Nicole said.

"We've hit up our usual donors too much already," Simeon pointed out. "We have to make this happen ourselves."

As April captured several of the ideas she, Simeon and Nicole discussed with her dry-erase marker, she noticed LaDonna thumbing through documents in the worn leather messenger bag she always carried around.

"Hello, Ms. Director," April directed toward La-Donna. "You mind giving a little input?"

Without saying a word, LaDonna slipped a sheaf of papers from the messenger bag and rose from her spot on the couch. She walked over to the whiteboard, picked up the eraser and swiped it back and forth across the list April had written.

Before April could shout the *girl, what you doing?* that was on the tip of her tongue, LaDonna held up the documents.

"This is all the funding we need," their director said.

"Is that like a secret code to winning the lottery?" Nicole asked with a laugh.

"And now we all know why you're a dancer and not a comedian," LaDonna said. "It's a new grant being offered by the state, in conjunction with a federal program through the Department of Education. It's specifically targeted to after-school, weekend and summer programs in impoverished areas."

"That's us," Simeon said.

"It's also highly selective. If we can prove that A Fresh Start is worthy of a grant, we won't have to worry about piecemealing our budget together with bake sales or online crowd-funding campaigns."

April lifted the document from LaDonna's fingers and flipped through it. "So, how do we go about getting the grant?"

"We make sure we can check off every single criterion listed here, and then we come up with our own set of criteria so that A Fresh Start can stand out."

April could only stare in amazement as she skimmed over the items the grant would provide. This was it. It was everything they needed.

"Why haven't you mentioned this to us before?" she asked LaDonna.

"Because I thought I could do it on my own." The director held a finger up to April. "Don't say anything. I'm here sharing it with you all now, okay?" She released a sigh. "I'm learning to ask for help, so stop judging me and let's work on getting this grant."

"Fine, I'll judge you later," April said. "Forget everything else. Including the alcohol," she said to Simeon as he drained his beer bottle. "We need to stay focused so that we can come up with the best way to earn this grant."

They had to. There was too much at stake for them to fail.

Damien Alexander winced as his tire bounced in the unavoidable pothole. It was even deeper than he'd gauged, and caused dirty water to splash all the way up to the driver's side window of his freshly washed Mercedes M-Class.

"Dammit," he cursed under his breath.

He swerved again, trying to avoid another crater, but it was nearly impossible in this part of the city. He remembered New Orleans winning the dubious title of the most potholes in a major city a few years ago. It was a wonder it didn't win every single year.

Damien took a right onto Lamanche, driving several blocks down the street that was less than a mile from the house where he grew up in the Lower Ninth Ward.

Damn, but he didn't want to be here. He'd rather be anywhere else *but* here.

When April returned his text with instructions to meet up with her at A Fresh Start, he'd wanted to reply with a counteroffer. But asking her to drive out to downtown New Orleans or closer to where he lived uptown wasn't fair, especially when he was the one who needed a favor from her.

Still, Damien resented having to come into this part of the city. The memories this place evoked were not happy ones.

The indiscriminate tan brick building across from Saint Katherine's Catholic Church came into view. The church must have something going on because every parking spot was filled.

Damien made the block, trying to find street parking, but came up empty. As he rounded the building again, he spotted a car pulling out about three spots from the entrance. He parallel parked the Mercedes on the street, engaging the alarm system before taking off for the building.

The boisterous clamor of several dozen teen voices hit him as soon as he opened the doors to the single-story structure that housed A Fresh Start. April had previously explained that the building was once a small Catholic school affiliated with the church. When the school closed years ago, the building then became the church's offices and community center, but its congregation had dwindled to the point where the extra space was unnecessary. The parish of Saint Katherine's had generously offered the community-based summer program use of the building at an affordable rent.

There had been nothing like A Fresh Start when Damien had been a young boy running roughshod through the streets of this neighborhood. He hoped these kids appreciated the sacrifice and hard work of April and the other volunteers who ran the program.

He walked down the single corridor, peering into the various rooms where everything from a cooking demonstration to arts and crafts was being held. The hauntingly sweet notes of string instruments guided him toward the rear of the building. He stopped at the open doorway of a room with about a dozen students, each holding some kind of instrument.

April Knight crouched next to a girl who sat with a cello positioned between her spaced knees. The large, slightly scarred instrument dwarfed her, but the teen didn't seem intimidated. She looked on intently as, with her signature calmness, April corrected whatever misstep the girl had just made on the piece they were practicing. She instructed her on how to glide the bow along the taut strings. The result was a fluid, mesmerizing note that resonated throughout the space.

Once she was done assisting the room's lone cello

player, April returned to the front of the room. When she turned and spotted him, her face lit up with a smile. Several of the students—those who were not engrossed in reading their sheet music—turned to see who had captured their teacher's attention. April held up a hand and mouthed *five minutes*.

Damien nodded. Leaning a shoulder along the door-jamb, he folded his arms across his chest, crossed his ankles and studied the woman standing at the helm of the class. It had been months since he'd seen her, not since running into her at a Christmas party that one of his clients had invited him to at a loft in the Warehouse District. That had been what? Six months ago?

He'd arrived late, and April had been on her way out. Their encounter had been nothing more than a quick hug and profuse thanks from April for the donation Damien had given to A Fresh Start. They both promised each other that they would meet for coffee so they could catch up, but whenever he'd thought about calling her over the past six months something else always came up.

Five minutes came and went, but Damien didn't dare interrupt April as she coached her pupils through a delicate piece. Besides, watching her in action was too entertaining to bring it to an end.

And to Damien's surprise he was watching her with more interest than he ever remembered watching his friend before. She wore soft yellow capri pants that hit just past her calves, a smart choice on this warm day. She probably had the heat and humidity in mind when she chose to pair it with the white sleeveless button-down blouse, but Damien thought it was the right choice for an entirely different reason.

He studied the way she moved, her toned arms slicing the air as she directed the young musicians. Years of playing the cello had added definition to her muscles, which still managed to look delicate underneath her smooth skin. Her warm brown complexion looked radiant despite the harsh fluorescent lighting above. Her shoulder-length hair had been swept up in a messy bun atop her head, accenting those cheekbones that had always been her most standout feature.

Although, to be honest, everything about her seemed to stand out to him today.

April finally brought the class to an end, instructing the students to properly stow their instruments so that they would be ready for the next class. Once all students had vacated the room, she came up to Damien and wrapped him up in a big hug.

"Long time no see," she said.

Damien returned the hug, discovering that the toned muscles applied to more than just her arms. That delicate thing she had going on was definitely a facade.

"Thanks for making time for me today," Damien returned.

"Of course," April said. "So, how has it been going, Mr. Bachelor of the Year?"

Damien's head fell back as he released a strained breath. "Please, don't start." He looked at her again, one brow pitched upward. "And it isn't Bachelor of the Year."

"Oh, that's right. You're just *one* of New Orleans's top ten bachelors. My bad."

"Are you finished?" Damien asked. "Or do you want to rub this in just a little more? It's okay, I can handle anything you dish out."

"Aw," April said. "Been a rough one, has it? Okay," she said, "I promise no more bachelor jokes for the next hour."

"An entire hour? You're such a giver, April."

She laughed again, the sound echoing around the empty room. She grabbed him by the cuff of his light blue button-down and tugged.

"Come on, let's get some coffee. The new café is finally operational and I cannot wait for you to see it."

"You were able to make it happen?" Damien asked.

"Along with the kids and other volunteers, of course. But, yes, we made it happen. Thanks in no small part to donations from generous citizens such as yourself," she said. She stopped and turned. "Did I tell you that I found a college in northern Mississippi that was replacing all of their string instruments?" She pointed over her shoulder, toward the room they'd just left. "Those violins and the double bass you saw the kids playing? All purchased with the money you donated. I can't thank you enough, Damien."

Damien could only hope that her giving spirit would still be there when he brought up the reason for his visit.

"Here it is," April said as they arrived at the newly installed coffee bar and café.

Damien looked around the room, a grin slowly lifting up the corner of his mouth. The building's rearmost room had been converted into a small eatery. A long counter ran nearly the entire length of the back wall. Behind it sat an industrial espresso/cappuccino maker and a professional blender. Three stainless steel pump-style coffee dispensers labeled Decaf, Medium Roast and Dark Roast sat on the counter next to glass domes that housed various pastries.

There were five small round tables inside, each with a small vase holding a single bud in their center, and two chairs. Just outside, on the brick patio on the rear eastern side of the building, sat three additional seating areas. There also looked to be a small vegetable garden just beyond it.

"You know, when you called asking for a donation from Alexander Properties to help fund this project, I pictured something that was a step above a lemonade stand. But this is a legitimate coffee shop." He glanced over at April. "I guess I should have known better. When it comes to April Knight, there's never any half stepping."

"You got that right," April said with a sharp nod, followed by that infectious laugh of hers.

When she'd approached him at the end of last summer with the idea for the café, she told him that she wanted it to serve two purposes. First, she assured him that it would be operated strictly by the youth who attended A Fresh Start and used foremost as a teaching tool, giving the kids practical skills that they could use to hopefully gain employment outside the center. And, second, the money provided from the sales would be used to fund other programs.

Damien purchased two large black coffees, leaving a twenty-dollar tip in the tip jar, then followed April to the lone available table.

"It looks as if you all have a bustling business already," Damien commented as he sat across from her. "Not an empty seat in the house."

"It's a symbiotic relationship. This community needed something like this," April said. "And the kids love it.

We—" She paused, looking beyond Damien. "Hey, Simeon, what's up?"

Damien looked over his shoulder just as a young guy of about twenty-five or so came upon their table. He wore a plaid shirt and slim jeans with cuffs that rolled up above his ankles.

"Sorry to interrupt," the guy said. "I just wanted to know what time I'm meeting you at your house."

A dose of unease slithered through Damien's bones.

Was April dating this guy? Why hadn't he considered the possibility that she was in a relationship before coming up with his hastily hatched plan?

"Be there for seven," April told the youngster.

"Awesome. See you then," he answered, and then left them.

April took a sip of coffee and said, "Sorry about that. Now, what is it that's so urgent that it brought you to the Ninth Ward? Don't think that the significance of this visit escaped my attention. It's been a long time since you came out this way."

"Yeah, it has," Damien said. "First, are you seeing someone?"

Her head jerked back as she released a shocked laugh. "What?"

"You know, romantically," Damien said. "Are you involved with someone?"

He knew he'd caught her off guard. He and April had been friends since high school, but their love lives were rarely discussed. In fact, Damien couldn't remember either of them ever overtly bringing up the subject.

"I…uh…" She stumbled. Then shook her head. "No," she finally answered. "No, I'm not seeing anyone."

Bone-melting relief replaced that earlier unease.

"Great," Damien said. "Because I have a favor to ask of you. And it's a big one."

April didn't know what to think as she watched Damien fidget across the table from her. If there was one thing she could usually say about him, it was that he excelled at always appearing to be completely in control.

Not today.

Right now, he seemed unsure. Nervous, even. It was unsettling.

Damien tapped his fingers on the table in an anxious rhythm. "The reason I asked you to meet with me—" he started.

"Hi. Can I get you anything?" Jelissa Cannon, one of the older girls who helped to manage the new café, interrupted.

The teen flashed a huge smile at Damien. Like most of the world's female population, she seemed totally smitten within a second of setting eyes on him.

April held up her cup. "We already have our drinks, but thanks."

"Oh." Jelissa's smile deflated. Then it brightened again. "Can I get you anything else? Refills, maybe?"

Did that child just bat her eyes?

"Actually, I think we're good for now," April answered, infusing a hint of warning into her voice.

"Are you sure?" Jelissa asked Damien.

"Yes," Damien said, treating her to that megawatt smile that had no choice but to elicit the exact reaction Jelissa displayed. The teen giggled like the schoolgirl she was, her light brown cheeks darkening to a deep crimson.

"If we need refills, I'll call you over," April told her. She wiggled her fingers toward the counter. "You have customers to take care of. Why don't you go and do that?"

April cast a cursory glance around the room and discovered that Jelissa wasn't the only one with eyes trained on their table. Most of the females in the room were staring openly at them.

It wasn't as if April could blame them. If there was one thing Damien Alexander had always been, it was easy on the eyes.

April had done her share of looking over the years.

Oh, who was she kidding? She'd nearly sprained her eyes staring at him.

She could remember the way her skin tingled that very first day she saw him, back when the two of them first met as sophomores at George Washington Carver High School. His features had become more refined over the years, but that strong jaw and chin, those thick eyebrows over whiskey-brown eyes, and that sensual dip in his lip had been there from the very beginning. Many a girl had fallen under the spell of those arresting features. Herself included.

Thankfully, April knew better than to act on it.

Oh, she could still appreciate the sheer devastating beauty that was Damien Alexander, but April had managed to tamp down her lustful thoughts where her friend was concerned. While other women openly stared, making downright fools of themselves, she was content to just eye him from afar. It became obvious over the years that she and Damien would always be friends, but nothing more. April had come to both accept and respect that.

Wait, she hadn't noticed any pigs flying in the sky on her way in here this morning, had she?

Okay, so maybe she wasn't completely accepting of her relationship with Damien. Or, her lack of a relationship, as it was. But at least she no longer pined for him as she had when they were younger. She would eventually be at peace with the idea of being nothing but a friend. It's just that the road to peace was long and unwieldy.

April turned her attention back to Damien. "Before we get to the reason you're here, you must tell me how this top ten bachelor thing came about."

Damien released an agitated sigh. "Must we?"

"We must," April answered. "Now spill it. I want to know who managed to talk you into posing for that picture."

When she'd opened her copy of *Get to Know NOLA* magazine last week and spotted that picture of Damien in a suit that fit him to perfection, she'd nearly fallen off her kitchen chair. She'd managed to stop herself from tearing it out of the magazine and framing it, but just barely.

"Can't we talk about this later?" Damien asked.

"Nope. I want the skinny."

His annoyed look didn't deter April one bit. One of the benefits—if one could call it that—of being a platonic friend was that she could get away with pushing his buttons. Damien ran a hand down his goatee and took another sip of his black coffee. "This is good, by the way," he said, holding up the cup.

"Thanks. I'll make sure the kids know you said so. Now out with it."

"Bossy, as usual," Damien said. He took another sip

of coffee before continuing. "Someone at the magazine contacted me out of the blue a couple of months ago. And you know me—I'm never one to turn down free publicity, so I said yes. I never thought it would take off the way it did. I mean, who even reads *Get to Know NOLA* magazine?"

April raised her hand. "I've been a faithful reader since it launched a couple of years ago, and after that photo spread, I'll bet there will be a lot more people reading it. Whoever came up with the top ten bachelors idea is a genius. It's gone viral. You should be happy, you're getting the publicity you wanted."

"No." Damien shook his head. "This is *not* the publicity I wanted. This is the exact opposite of what I wanted. When I agreed to do that photo shoot, I thought it would be a way to bring attention to my business. That's why I insisted the shoot happen in my office instead of out on the lakefront where they first suggested. The goal was for Alexander Properties to get some action, not me."

"Because you've got all the action you can handle, right?" April asked.

It was no secret he'd had his share of beautiful women. It had been that way throughout high school. And even though they'd seen each other only sparingly over the past decade, Damien never failed to have some gorgeous beauty on his arm.

"I'm not in the market for that kind of action right now. Being involved with a woman is a complication I don't have time for," he said. "That's why I'm here to see you."

"I'll try not to be offended," she drawled.

He grimaced. "That didn't come out right."

"Forget about it," April said with a wave of her hand. It wasn't as if she didn't know where she stood. "What exactly is it that you need?"

"Let me see if I can set this up for you," he said. He spread his fingers out over the table. "I hadn't mentioned anything prior to today because I wasn't sure if this was going to go through or not. But it did go through, so I can finally talk about it."

"Can you be any more vague?"

"Have you always been such a smart-ass?"

"Only when it's warranted," April answered. "What is the *it* that you can finally talk about?"

He tapped his fingers on the table, revealing a hint of that nervousness she'd sensed in him earlier.

April reached across the table and covered his hand. "Damien, what's this all about? It isn't like you to beat around the bush this way."

"There's a huge abandoned lot around North Galvez and Kentucky Streets, not too far from the train tracks."

"Yeah, I know it. There's still some blighted houses that way, and a bunch of overgrown lawns," she said.

"Yeah, that's it. Well, I own all of it now."

April's mouth scrunched up with confusion. "Why?"

"I'm in real estate, April. That's what I do."

"Yeah, but you're in corporate real estate. Do you really think you can convince any of your clients to move their companies from the Central Business District to the Ninth Ward?"

"I have something else in mind for that property," Damien said. "Something that can potentially be a game changer. But I can't do it on my own. Alexander Properties does okay, but I'm still small potatoes when it comes to the kind of capital I'll need to pull this off. It'll require other investors—several of them—if I'm going to get this project off the ground. And that's where you come in?"

April's brow arched. "Just in case you've forgotten, you're the one I come to when A Fresh Start needs some cash," she said. "I'm just a lowly musician, getting work where I can find it."

"Yeah, right. You're turning down work left and right," Damien said.

That was true. She'd just turned down an offer with an orchestra in Thailand.

"But that's not the kind of help I need from you," Damien said. He took another swig of coffee, set the cup back on the table then took both of her hands in his.

With an intense stare directly into her eyes, he said, "I need you to be my girlfriend."

Chapter 2

April's mouth dropped opened.

Seconds stretched between them as she continued to stare at him, her expression unreadable.

"Let me explain," Damien said.

"Uh, yes," she said. "Maybe you should."

But before Damien could elaborate, there was a huge crash on the other side of the room. He and April both jumped. He looked over his shoulder and spotted one of the small round café tables on its side. Two girls were going at it, arms and thick hair braids swinging.

A group of kids swarmed the girls, egging them on, yelling, "Fight! Fight!"

Damien jumped up from his seat, but before he could break up the fight, April was already there. She stepped in between the two girls, her arms splayed wide, her chest heaving with the deep breaths she pulled in.

"Break it up! Break. It. Up," April said.

The girl with the deep purple hair braids took another swing, nearly clipping April's face.

Damien took an automatic step toward them, but April held him back with a hand.

"I've got this," she said. She pointed at the crowd of kids still surrounding them. "The rest of you, get back to wherever you're supposed to be right now. If it's the café, find somewhere else to be until I say you can return."

She turned to the girls who had been fighting. Bracing both hands on her hips, April blasted them with a glare that made Damien want to take a step back.

"What's going on here?" she asked.

Silence followed.

The glare intensified. "Someone had better start talking. You're only making it worse on yourselves."

Still, silence ensued.

Damien noticed the first chink in her armor as she looked at the girls, who now both stood with their heads bowed, staring at the floor. April's crestfallen expression showed him how hard this was for her.

"Dammit, Cressida and Makayla," April said. "You both know there is a zero-tolerance policy when it comes to fighting."

"You're going to kick us out?" the girl with normal-colored hair asked.

"Do you understand what zero tolerance means?" April asked her. "It means that if you do not abide by the rules, you do not get to stay. End of story."

"But, Ms. April," the girl started, but April stopped her. She put her hand up.

"It's not my call. Ms. LaDonna will make all deci-

sions. Go to her office and explain what this fight was
about. She will decide whether or not you both deserve
to stay."

Their heads hanging, the girls lumbered away as if
part of a funeral procession.

A round of applause broke out around the room from
the patrons who occupied the other tables.

April released a weary laugh and bowed, accepting
their praise.

"I'm sorry for the interruption," she said in a voice
that carried around the room.

She turned to Damien. She looked as if she'd just
gone ten rounds with a heavyweight fighter, though he
sensed that her exhaustion had more to do with those
girls potentially getting kicked out of the program than
the physical exertion of breaking up the fight.

"How often are you required to play referee?" Damien
asked.

"Thankfully, not that often," she said. "This is only
the second fight this year. It's a part of my job that I'm
not all that fond of, but it has to be done."

"You do it well," Damien said. "Of course, you had
practice. So maybe I should take some credit after all."

"Oh, believe me, I remember," April said with a laugh.

She'd been witness to many of the skirmishes Damien
had found himself in while growing up in these streets.
She'd never gotten in the middle of them the way she
had today, but afterward, while she helped clean whatever scrapes he'd amassed during the fight, she would
let him know how disappointed she was in him. It was
the knowledge that he disappointed her that eventually
quelled Damien's desire to engage in that kind of be-
havior.

April Knight made him want to be a better person. She always had.

"Will those girls really be kicked out of the program?" Damien asked as they returned to their table.

She nodded. "For the rest of the summer. They can apply to gain entrance next summer."

"So A Fresh Start actually adheres to its zero-tolerance policy, huh?"

"It wasn't always that way," April said with a laugh. "Let's just say that I'm not the only sucker for puppy-dog eyes and apologies around here. We have a staff full of bleeding hearts, but once we noticed that the amount of infractions was increasing instead of decreasing, we finally put our collective feet down.

"We've discovered that a strictly enforced zero-tolerance policy is a lot more effective than paying lip service. And the more activities we add to the program, the more it makes kids want to stick to the rules so they can continue to participate."

April folded her hands one on top of the other, and said, "So, exactly what were you saying before we were interrupted?"

Damien nodded. "As I mentioned before, Alexander Properties now owns a large square of real estate in the Lower Ninth Ward, but in order to develop it I'll need investors. There are several social events happening over the summer that will put me in the same space with some of the New Orleans area's most prominent business owners. The key word in all of that is *social*."

"Okay," April said, dragging the word out. "And I fit in where?"

"I don't want to show up stag at any of these events, but I also don't want to deal with any messy relationship crap. This top ten bachelor thing will just make it worse. My focus has to be on business, not on worrying about whether or not my date is entertained."

April sat back in her chair and folded her arms across her chest.

"Is this the sales pitch you prepared? Because if so, you suck at this selling thing. I'm surprised your business is as successful as it is."

Damien put both hands up. "Okay, so maybe that didn't come out exactly the way I thought it would."

"Let me see if I understand," April said. "You basically want me to be a warm body in a pretty dress who can fend off other women so that you can concentrate on business."

Damien's shoulders lifted in a hapless shrug. "Basically, yeah."

She caught the lone sugar packet on the table and flipped it between her fingers. "Why me?" April asked. "If there is one area where you are not lacking, it's the old girlfriend department. At least one of those relationships had to have ended amicably enough for you to call in a favor."

"If I asked any of my old girlfriends, they would take it the wrong way, probably thinking that I wanted a reconciliation or something." He looked over at her, hoping to infuse as much pleading into his expression as possible. "Please, April. I promise not to take up too much of your time. We're talking three to four events, tops. Maybe five if I'm able to score tickets to the charity auction for the Children's Hospital."

"You don't expect me to answer right away, do you?"

Actually, he had. Kinda.

"No," Damien said, shaking his head. "I figured

you'd need some time to think about it. It's just that, um, the first event is Friday night, so I'll need to know pretty soon."

Damien reached over and covered the hand that still toyed around with the sugar packet. He gave it a light squeeze.

"Please, April," he pleaded. "At least think about it. And then say yes."

Several moments stretched between them before she said, "I'll think about it. I've got another music class starting in a few minutes, so I need to go, but I'll get back to you later today."

Damien stood, a smile drawing across his face. "I guess that'll have to be good enough for now," he said. He leaned over and placed a kiss on her cheek. "I'll talk to you later. Thanks for considering this, April."

He winked at her, then started for the exit, feeling a whole lot better than he had when he'd first walked through these doors.

I need you to be my girlfriend.

Her stupid heart gave a stupid leap of joy as April replayed Damien's words in her mind, even after discovering just what he'd meant by that. He needed her to be his *fake* girlfriend. A pretend love interest. A phony plaything he could drape on his arm so that he wouldn't have to deal with any of the women who—if he were not tied up with this special project of his—would actually be candidates to be his *real* girlfriend. Damn him for giving her those few brief seconds of hope.

She snapped the lid closed on the violin case with more force than necessary.

"You're an idiot," April said with a disgruntled sigh.

"But at least you broke up that fight today before any limbs were lost, so you're not completely pathetic."

"You talking to yourself again?"

April yelped and swung around, finding Nicole standing in the doorway.

"Girl!" April yelled, holding her hand to her chest.

"Sorry." Nicole laughed. "I couldn't help it." The twenty-five-year-old sauntered into the room where April had just finished up her intermediate music class. Nicole grabbed the handles of two of the violin cases and followed April to the closet where the instruments were stored at the end of the day.

"Thanks," April said over her shoulder. She locked the door then turned to find Nicole standing there with her arms crossed.

"So," Nicole said, a cagey smile tipping up the corners of her lips. "Looks as if you've been holding out on us."

"I have? How so?" She gathered the last of the sheet music into a pile and used the mug from her desk as a paperweight.

"Uh, *hellooo*!" Nicole sang. "Was that not Damien Alexander who came to see you today? You never told me that you knew him."

April tilted her head to the side and touched her finger to her chin. "Funny, but I can't recall telling you even a tenth of the people I know. I'm not sure why I would tell you about Damien."

"Whatever," Nicole said with an eye roll to rival those of the teens who walked the halls. "So, how do you know him? More importantly, how *well* do you know him, if you catch my drift." She lifted her eyebrows suggestively.

"Get your mind out of the gutter," April said with a laugh. "Damien and I went to high school together. We've been friends for years."

"So you're just friends?"

"Just friends," April said. "Nothing more."

She would ignore the pang of disappointment that attempted to seep into her skin.

"Awesome," Nicole said. "That means you wouldn't have a problem introducing me to him."

"Believe me, the one thing Damien isn't looking for right now is to be introduced to a woman. In fact, that's the exact opposite of what he wants."

"Don't tell me he's gay," Nicole said in a shocked voice.

April barked out a laugh. "No, he isn't. He just has no interest in dating right now."

"So he came to see you? Yikes."

"I already told you that we're friends. There's no reason for me to be upset or offended."

So what if most women would be offended if a handsome, sought-after bachelor called on them because they were not interested in getting involved with anyone. She was bigger than that, wasn't she?

No. No, she was not.

But she would save the wall-kicking and raging at the ceiling for tonight, when she was in the sanctuary of her own home with copious amounts of chocolate, wine and *Nurse Jackie* binge watching to keep her company.

"Whatever you say," Nicole said. "Oh, I'm doubling up on my hip-hop dance class tomorrow because a bunch of the kids are going to Saint Michael's Youth Day thing on Friday."

"Oh, that's this weekend?"

"Yeah, there's a bus bringing them over to the North-shore."

"Hi, ladies." LaDonna stuck her head in the door. "I heard Damien Alexander stopped in today. Is he still here?"

April threw her hands in the air. "Oh, for crying out loud. Did someone send out a group text as soon as he walked through the door?"

"It was a Snapchat video," LaDonna said, coming into the room. "Get with the times."

"I don't even know what Snapchat is," April said. She barely remembered to check her Facebook page. "But, to answer your question, no, Damien isn't here. He had to get back to his office. He was only here because he wanted to ask a favor of me."

"I'm sorry I missed seeing him," LaDonna said. "I would have liked to thank him personally for his donation last year."

"Too bad you missed it. He was something to see," Nicole said, fanning herself.

April rolled her eyes. "Don't you have to go break Simeon's heart again?"

"Hey," Nicole said with affront. "It's not my fault he's still trying even after I told him I wasn't interested."

"Maybe if you weren't giving him all these mixed signals," April said.

"I do not!"

"Yes, you do," April and LaDonna said at the same time.

"Case in point, the meeting at my house the other night," April said. "I know my living room isn't big, but don't you think you could have found somewhere else to sit? There was no need for you to plant your behind right next to him on the floor."

Nicole's lips scrunched up in a frown. "Fine. No more mixed signals. But it shouldn't count if I don't even realize I'm doing it."

LaDonna put a hand up. "I'm tired of this conversation. Back to Damien Alexander. How well do you know him?" she asked April.

"Well enough. We went to high school together. I used to tutor him in English."

LaDonna perched her hip on the desk. "This may be just wishful thinking on my part, but do you think there's any chance you can get him to join us here at A Fresh Start?"

"As in…?"

"As in volunteering," LaDonna said.

April shook her head. "He has a business to run. He can't—"

"I know he's busy," LaDonna said, cutting her off. "And I'm not talking about full-time, everyday volunteering. I'm talking about an hour a week, maybe on Saturday mornings.

"I've been reading all these blogs about ways to increase your chances of winning a grant, and having a well-rounded program seems to be key. We have a nice assortment of recreational programs for the kids, but think of how it would look on our grant application if we had a prominent businessman teaching the kids about money management."

"A money management class?"

"Think about it," LaDonna said. "We're teaching them job skills with the new café and there are a number of the older kids who have part-time jobs this summer. But many of them don't know anything about savings or taxes. These are life skills."

April couldn't deny that it was definitely needed. Just yesterday she'd had to explain what FICA was to a group of kids who were comparing their first pay stubs. Rashad Parker said he'd borrowed money to buy a new video game from his uncle based on his hourly wage, not realizing that he wouldn't get the entire amount in his paycheck.

This foray into the work world was a first for many of the kids there. They had a lot to learn, and Damien was well equipped to teach them.

But to convince Damien to come out to the Ninth Ward on a weekly basis?

April still couldn't believe he'd made the trek to this part of town this morning. He may have purchased land here, but she knew better than to think it would change his feelings about their old neighborhood. Damien had deep-rooted disdain for this area, and for good reason. These streets had taken an awful toll on his family.

She'd tried to explain to him over the two years since they'd both returned to New Orleans that this neighborhood had changed for the better, yet it was as if he suddenly lost his hearing whenever she started. He supported her efforts to make a difference in the lives of the kids who lived here; however, donating money seemed to be the extent of what he was willing to do. April doubted she could ever convince Damien to voluntarily spend time here.

Unless…

A smile tipped up the corners of April's lips. Why hadn't she thought of this before?

"Give me a day or two, ladies. I just might have the perfect way to convince Damien Alexander to volunteer at A Fresh Start."

* * *

April made a left onto South Peters and then a quick right, driving up to the towering parking garage at One Canal Place. She knew Alexander Properties was located in the high-rise at the base of Canal Street, but it wasn't until she'd had to look it up on Google to find the suite number that it occurred to April that, in the two years since Damien moved his real estate firm from Houston to New Orleans, she hadn't once visited his office.

High-end retailers, the ones she used to patronize back when she played some of the most prestigious music halls in the world and was required to wear ball gowns to work, occupied the first two floors of the building. April much preferred her current dress code.

The elevator bank that led to the attached office building was packed with business-attired people all staring intently at the descending numbers above the elevator doors. April would have taken the stairs if Damien weren't on the very top floor. Although, considering the amount of people waiting for the elevator, it would probably take the same amount of time to reach his office.

After seeing three elevators come and go before she could finally squeeze into one, April still had to wait through more than a dozen stops as they ascended to the thirty-first floor.

She should be grateful for the long trek to Damien's office. It gave her time to mull over the proposition she would soon present to him. April was fully prepared for Damien to send her marching out of his office—figuratively, at least. Even though he said he didn't want to go the ex-girlfriend route, she knew he had his pick of other women he could call on to accompany him to events this summer.

But she'd sensed desperation in his eyes when he'd come to see her at A Fresh Start this morning. Something in the way he'd pleaded with her said that this went deeper than just having a woman on his arm. April planned to make that desperation work to her advantage.

She was the elevator's sole occupant by the time it arrived on the top floor. She made her way down the hallway to the suite bearing the Alexander Properties logo, with the capital *A* and *P* overlapping. April allowed herself to indulge in a moment of pride. She'd helped Damien pick this logo five years ago, when he branched off from the national real estate firm he'd worked for since graduating from college and started his own company.

The door opened before she could reach for the handle, and a plump Melissa McCarthy lookalike with hot-pink horn-rimmed glasses and bright red lipstick came out.

"Oh, hello there," she greeted. "Can I help you?"

"Yes, I'm here to see Damien Alexander," April said.

The woman's eyes narrowed in suspicion, and it occurred to April that this office might have experienced an uptick in women showing up at the door to see Damien since the release of that top ten bachelors article.

"Oh!" The woman snapped her fingers. "Now I remember who you are! You're on that magazine cover."

April's head jerked back in surprise. "Me?"

"Yeah. You're the cellist. Ms. Knight, right?"

"Yes. April," she said.

The woman held out her hand. "I'm Clarissa, the office

manager here. You were on the cover of some classical-music magazine a few years back. Damien has a copy he keeps on the credenza in his office."

April's heart skipped a beat. An array of emotions cascaded through her at the thought of Damien holding on to a copy of the obscure magazine she'd been featured in years ago. She didn't realize he'd even run across it, seeing as only true classical music devotees normally read it.

Clarissa held up a finger. "Give me just one sec." She looked past April. "Hi, Ryan."

A young blond guy in his early twenties walked toward them, a bicycle helmet tucked under one arm and a messenger bag slung over his shoulder. Right Away Courier Services was embroidered across the front flap.

Clarissa signed the form attached to a clipboard, then took the sealed envelope that was handed to her. "Thanks, Ryan. I'll see you again next week."

She stared at the blond as he retreated down the hallway, her eyes clearly focused on a certain part of his anatomy.

Clarissa clucked her tongue. "God, I love summer. The khaki pants just don't fit him as well as those butt-hugging shorts do." She nodded toward the door. "Follow me. Damien's on a conference call but he should be done in a minute."

Upon entering the office, April declined a seat on the white suede-like love seat, choosing instead to stand while she perused the sparse yet elegant lobby area. The receptionist's desk was a huge semicircle that encompassed most of the small entryway, done in what looked like the aluminum roofing that was used on older houses when April was growing up. It was topped with beautiful jade-tinted frosted glass.

April was a bit surprised by the decor. She'd pegged Damien as one who would prefer rich, dark wood over glass-and-steel ultramodern furnishings. But then it occurred to her that she had not spent enough time with him over the years to know if this was his style or not.

The realization caused a pang of sadness to ring through her. Their lives had turned out so differently from those teenage fantasies she used to indulge in, back when she imagined herself and Damien married with two-point-five kids, living in a nice house in Old Metairie or in Algiers Point. She'd imagined herself as a member of the Louisiana Philharmonic Orchestra while Damien played football for the New Orleans Saints.

At least she'd had the opportunity to perform as a soloist with the LPO at Gallier Hall years ago. It was the closest she'd come to living out at least one part of those long-ago dreams.

Clarissa disconnected from the call she'd taken the moment they walked into the office.

"Let me buzz Damien for you," she said. "His conference call should have ended by now."

"If he's busy, I can wait. I don't have an appointment, so I don't want to infringe on his time if he's in the middle of something."

And wouldn't that be a great excuse to back out of the deal she was preparing to propose?

Clarissa nodded as she spoke into the small microphone attached to her headset.

Moments later, Damien rounded the wall that led to the lobby area.

"Hey," he greeted April with a curious lift to his brow. "Did I miss a text from you or something?"

"No, no. I'm sorry for not calling first, but I'm hoping I can steal a few minutes of your time."

"Do you have an answer to the favor I asked for earlier?" he asked, hopefulness pushing away that earlier curiosity.

"I do," April said. She looked over at Clarissa, who was blatantly hanging on to every word. "Is there somewhere we can go to discuss it?"

Damien's eyes flashed to his receptionist. "Yeah, sure," he said. "We can go to my office."

April followed him into a spacious office done in the same modern furnishings as the rest of the suite. He pointed to a small sitting area. "Have a seat. Can I get you some coffee? Water?"

"No, thanks," April said.

He poured himself a cup of water from a glass pitcher.

"Okay, so are you going to help me out?" Damien asked.

April clasped her hands and released a deep breath before saying, "Yes, I will." Relief washed over Damien's face. "But, there's a catch," she tacked on.

His relief turned to suspicion. "A catch?"

"Maybe *catch* is the wrong word," she said. "Think of it as an agreement between the two of us. You'll get what you want, and I will get what I want."

"Why do I sense a Knight ambush coming on?" Damien asked.

"There is no such thing as a Knight ambush," April countered.

"Are you serious? You're the queen of ambushes.

Do you remember all those surprise study sessions you used to spring on me? They still give me nightmares."

"But those study sessions helped you in the end, didn't they?"

The corner of his mouth curled in that sexy little smile that made April's stomach flutter.

"Yeah, they did," Damien admitted. He perched his backside on the edge of the desk and crossed his feet at the ankles. "Okay, so what exactly is it that you want out of this bargain?"

"Let me just start out by saying that you've been an amazing financial contributor to A Fresh Start. Whenever I've asked you to donate, you've given without hesitating, and it goes without saying that the program wouldn't be the success it is today without the support of Alexander Properties and other local businesses like yours."

"Can we get to the catch?" Damien asked. "Not to rush you or anything, but I can actually feel myself growing older by the minute."

"Nice to know that sense of humor is still as abysmal as always," she said.

He laughed. "Come on, April. Just lay it out for me."

"Well, the financial support is wonderful, but it takes more than money to run a program like A Fresh Start. It takes warm bodies," she said. "And not just *any* warm bodies, but ones the kids can relate to."

His eyes narrowed. "You can't possibly mean me," Damien said.

"Of course I mean you," she said.

"You think a bunch of teenagers can relate to me? I don't even like kids."

"It doesn't matter how you feel about them now.

What matters is that you were a smart-mouthed knucklehead back when you were these kids' ages."

"So sweet of you to bring that up."

"I bring it up because you're not a knucklehead anymore, although that smart mouth seems to have remained." April rose from her chair and walked over to his desk. She leaned against it, mimicking his pose. "These kids need to see that someone who was once running the hundred-yard dash down the wrong path could change his life around so drastically. They need to see that there is a different way out of the Lower Ninth Ward besides being the next rapper or playing football."

"But it *was* football that initially got me out of there. Without football, I wouldn't have gotten that scholarship to Alcorn State."

"The scholarship was your foot in the door, but you worked your butt off to earn your degree."

"With the help of a certain music major helping me every step of the way," he said.

The gratitude in his words warmed her from the inside out.

"You were well worth the effort," April said. "And so are many of these kids."

He folded his arms across his chest. "So, what is it you want from me?"

"I want you to teach a course on money management at A Fresh Start. Nothing too intense, just something to start the kids on the right path when it comes to handling money. Many of them have summer jobs, and with the addition of the café, we're giving even more of them skills to make them employable. They need to learn the importance of not blowing all their hard-earned money all at once on payday."

Damien groaned. "Do you know how busy I am?"

"And you think I'm not? You want me to accompany you to all of these fancy events. Do you have any idea what that entails? I'll have to do hair, makeup, try on at least a half-dozen dresses until I decide to go with my first choice—"

He put his hands up. "Okay, okay."

"Everyone is busy, Damien. All I'm asking for is an hour of your time once a week for the next six weeks. Think about how valuable something like this would have been back when you had your first job bagging groceries at the Winn-Dixie supermarket."

He expelled the kind of put-out sigh that made it seem as if she were demanding his firstborn.

"Really, Damien, would it be so hard to give up just one hour a week? I'll even help plan the classes. In fact, I'll help you come up with a syllabus. I've been thinking about ideas since I left A Fresh Start. For example, I think some kind of game centered around investing would be fun—"

"Wait, wait, wait," Damien said, holding up both hands. "I haven't even agreed to do this yet."

"Okay," April said. "But you should know that if you want me to join you at all your little fancy shindigs, you have to teach the class."

His mouth fell open. "I can't believe you're really going to blackmail me."

"This isn't blackmail."

"Yes, it is. You refuse to help me unless I cave to your demands."

"This is a business negotiation, Damien. You should be well versed in how the game is played."

"Oh, I've played the game," he said. He started to

pace back and forth in front of her. "I just never thought my own friend would be my opponent."

"Well, think again," April said. "This class may play a key role in something we're planning for A Fresh Start, and if I have to blackmail you in order to make sure it happens, then that's what I'll do."

"I thought it wasn't blackmail?"

"Can we please stop fighting over semantics and get on with it? You're getting older by the minute, remember?"

Damien chuckled. "When did you get to be so feisty? I think I like this side of you, despite the fact that you're blackmailing me."

April ordered her cheeks not to blush, for all the good that did. She could feel her skin warming.

Damien finished off the water he'd poured earlier, then walked over to the credenza and refilled his glass. Turning back to face her, he slid one hand in his pocket and gestured toward her with his glass.

"Before I agree to this, I want to know about this plan of yours. What exactly would this class play a key role in?"

She hadn't planned on discussing the grant, but April realized it was easier to just put everything out there than to evade the conversation.

"We're putting together a grant proposal," she started. "LaDonna Miller, our director, stumbled upon this grant that provides government funding for community programs like A Fresh Start. We're hoping to turn A Fresh Start into a year-round program."

Damien's eyes widened. "I can't teach this seminar year-round. It's going to be hard enough to make time for it over the next six weeks."

"You don't have to teach it year-round," she said. "As long as we have your class as a part of the curriculum during the period when we file the paperwork—which will be in about a month—it will serve its purpose. We can always say that something came up and you had to pull out of the program. But it won't matter then because we'll already have the grant."

A smile drew across Damien's face. "Is Miss Goody-Two-Shoes actually considering lying on a grant application?"

"Stop it," April said. She could feel that damn blush making a return appearance. If anyone could make her skin flush, it was the man standing before her. He'd always had a horribly easy time of pushing her buttons.

"It wouldn't be a total lie as long as you don't tell me that you won't be able to continue teaching year round until *after* we file for the grant."

Damien let out a low, deep chuckle. "Do you know how adorable you are when you do that?"

She actively ignored the tingles that raced through her blood just at the thought of him thinking of her as adorable. Teddy bears were adorable. So were hamsters. Would she still get butterflies if he called her a hamster?

"When I do what?" April asked.

"When you try to justify doing anything that might seem remotely inappropriate." He pointed at her with the water glass again. "Remember when a bunch of us skipped school to go down to the Riverwalk? You said that you were helping the economy by supporting the local business, so it really wasn't that bad." He leaned forward, and in a hushed voice, said, "It's okay to walk on the wild side every now and then, April. It can even be fun."

Oh, forget it. There was no use in trying to ignore those tingles now. Not when she could physically feel his teasing voice flowing over her skin like warm honey. Why did he continue to have this effect on her after all these years?

"Are you going to accept my bargain, or what?"

"Not until we discuss *your* side of the bargain," he said. "Our first event is Friday."

"As in tomorrow night?" April asked.

He nodded.

"So you came to see me this morning knowing that the first event would be tomorrow night?"

"I wasn't sure if I'd be in town—I was originally scheduled to fly up to Minneapolis tomorrow morning, but the deal fell through. It's just as well. I'd rather attend the Art for Autism in the Warehouse District anyway. It's the unofficial kickoff of a string of summer fund-raising soirees."

"I'm pretty sure I heard about that. Isn't it a fundraiser to support autism awareness? They're asking everyone to wear blue, right?"

"Yes. One of the associates here has a son who suffers from the disorder, so Alexander Properties is already a supporter of the national nonprofit. However, tomorrow night's event isn't associated with the national group. It's the brainchild of a group of local activists. They're sectioning off several blocks of Julia Street, and all the museums and art galleries will be opened.

"I received word from a credible source that Michael Berger, a partner with the McGowan Group, will be there."

"The McGowan Group is the one that owns the

minor-league baseball franchise, right? What does he have to do with any of this?"

"You know about them?" Damien asked.

"I work for a nonprofit. Of course I know about them. They're huge philanthropists. Never mind the fact that they also own several fast-food franchises and hotels."

"Yes, they're huge proponents in building up the infrastructure of the city. They are the ones I'm targeting to invest in the project I have planned for the property I just bought in the Ninth Ward. In order to do so, I need someone like you—intelligent, cultured and non-clingy—on my arm."

Damien came to stand in front of her once again. "So, do we have a deal? I agree to teach the money management class for six weeks and you'll agree to be my date to these events for the same time frame?"

April stared at his outstretched hand, noticing the nicks and scratches marring his skin. He wore that tailored suit as though he'd been born in it, but one only had to look just below the surface to catch a glimpse of that rough-and-tumble boy who used to run the streets.

She wanted to spend time with that boy she used to know more than she would ever dare to admit. And he'd just given her a way to do so.

She clasped his hand.

"Deal."

Chapter 3

His hip perched upon the wide windowsill, Damien
rested an elbow against the double-paned glass as he
read over the purchase agreement for the row of crafts-
men duplexes he'd just acquired in the Broadmoor
neighborhood. He had contractors on standby, ready
to convert the three houses into office spaces. He even
had a small law practice on tap to move into the first
one. He'd emailed the lease agreement to the personal-
injury attorney as soon as the sale had gone through.

That was the kind of deal he lived for: quick and
uncomplicated. Unlike the deal he'd made with April
yesterday.

Damien tossed the purchase agreement on the credenza and turned to the window. He leaned forward,
resting his forehead on the thick glass. He softly tapped
his head against it in an attempt to knock loose some

of his common sense. Apparently, it was lodged somewhere up there.

How had he allowed himself to be coerced into spending his Saturday mornings in the Lower Ninth Ward? He'd spent the past two years since his return to New Orleans actively avoiding his old neighborhood. Yet he'd *volunteered* to teach a bunch of kids from the area about money management? Was he crazy?

But being forced to spend time in the Ninth Ward on a weekly basis for the next month and a half was only one part of it. In the hours since April left his office yesterday, Damien had discovered the other thing about this deal that had him on edge.

When he looked at April, he no longer saw the beanpole girl with braces and the thick French braid she used to wear in high school. To be honest, he hadn't seen her that way in a long time, but their get-togethers had been few and far between over the past decade. Usually, Damien saw her for only the length of one dinner, or sometimes just a quick coffee.

That was about to change. Drastically.

When he'd first devised this plan to use April as a deterrent for eager women wanting to get closer to one of New Orleans's top ten bachelors, Damien hadn't considered what it would be like to spend hours upon hours with her in a situation where they would be expected to be more than just friendly. He was about to find out just what that would entail, and it made him nervous.

Yet, at the same time, he was intrigued as hell.

There was a knock at his door only milliseconds before Clarissa's voice called, "Hey, are you ready?"

Damien's mind instantly switched back to business

mode as he turned away from the window. "Yes, I'm ready," he said. "Is everyone in the conference room?"

"Everyone but Mei. She's checking out that building at the corner of Clearview and Veterans. She texted to say that it looks good so far."

"Yes," Damien said with a fierce whisper, giving his fist a small pump in the air.

He'd had the old Horizons Bank and Trust building on his radar for months. Damien had a specific purpose in mind for it. With all the new films being shot in this area—which had been dubbed Hollywood South in recent years—he thought that building would be the perfect place for a new sound studio. His plans were to section it into various suites. One for audio and visual, another for editing, and the others for whatever else the film industry needed. He'd hired Mei Lui, a veteran of the film industry, to figure that out for him. He didn't care how it happened, as long as it did.

Damien grabbed his leather portfolio from his desk as he headed out of the office. "Do you mind bringing in a pot of coffee?" Damien asked his office manager.

"That's my job," Clarissa answered.

"Thanks," Damien replied as he entered the corner conference room.

His team of five real estate agents, two assistants and his financial guy were all seated around the glass conference table.

"We need to talk strategy about Alexander Quarters," Damien opened.

The name he'd picked for the building he wanted to erect on the land he'd purchased in the Ninth Ward had nothing to do with ego. Damien saw it as a way to honor his father. A memorial to a man who'd given his all to that neighborhood, including his life.

"I think there's something more important that we need to discuss first," Rajesh Singh, his senior financial analyst, said.

Damien's brow furrowed. There wasn't a single thing more important than Alexander Quarters. And why in the hell was the normally stoic Rajesh looking at him with that stupid grin on his face?

"We didn't realize we had one of New Orleans's top ten eligible bachelors in our midst," Rajesh said. "This needs to be discussed."

A round of applause broke out across the conference room, followed by a standing ovation.

"Oh, great," Damien muttered.

Clarissa entered the room with the requested coffee, along with a blueberry muffin sporting a handmade Top Bachelor sign stuck to the edge of a toothpick. Not requested.

"I wanted to put the little naked man we used on the cupcakes at my sister's bachelorette party, but *someone* told me that would be inappropriate for the workplace," Clarissa said, staring pointedly at Rajesh.

"I'm happy you listened," Damien said.

He decided to be a good sport about their good-natured ribbing, but after a few minutes—and some choice words from Clarissa for Damien lying about the reason the photographer was there weeks ago when he came to do the photo shoot for the article—Clarissa returned to her desk in reception and everyone got down to business.

"Our main focus remains the McGowan Group, but

you all have been working with me long enough to know that I need a plan B, C and D."

"No need to stop at D," Rajesh said. "Feel free to go through the entire alphabet."

Damien chuckled. "I promise not to go overboard this time. I feel confident about the McGowan Group, but it wouldn't hurt to have others on our radar in case things fall through." He turned to Sheryl Bardell, who'd followed him from the national real estate company where he'd first started out. "How are we doing when it comes to identifying the best events to attend where I can rub elbows with some of the city's top investors?" Damien asked.

"The stretch between the end of Mardi Gras and the beginning of football season is probably the best time to do this, so that's one notch in the plus column," Sheryl said. "They've recouped their money from carnival season, and the LSU and Tulane football boosters haven't been hit with requests from the schools yet."

Sheryl pressed a button on the remote she held and a bulleted list appeared on the projector screen on the far wall.

"We've identified a number of events around the city that should get you significant face time with potential investors. I think what we need to concentrate on is your pitch and, well, your appearance."

Damien's brows peaked again. "Excuse me?"

"I'm not talking about your appearance, per se, but rather how it would look to investors to have you showing up alone to all of these events. I know it sounds old-fashioned, but having a significant other on your arm conveys a sense of stability and loyalty. Both qualities investors look for."

"Don't worry about that," Damien said. "I've got it covered."

Silence encompassed the room.

"Since when?" Sheryl asked.

"Since yesterday," he answered.

"You found a girlfriend yesterday?" Rajesh asked.

"So you're no longer a bachelor?" This from Clarissa, who was listening through the speakerphone from her desk, which she did during meetings since the rest of them sucked at keeping minutes.

Damien picked up the coffee cup Clarissa had given him before going back to her desk and wrapped his hands around it. He put it back on the table without taking a sip.

"I approached a friend who happens to be a girl and asked her if she would accompany me to a few events," he said. "It's no big deal."

"You're so cute when you're trying to be humble," came Clarissa's voice through the phone speaker.

"Can we please get back to work and stop worrying about my dating life?" Damien asked.

The team spent the next twenty minutes discussing various deals coming down the pike, from those that were just in their infancy stages to potential buildings they all had their eyes on. Once the meeting ended, Damien went to his office and started sifting through his emails. He'd been so busy today that he hadn't had a chance to keep up with them on his phone.

"Damien, Leroy Fairchild just called to cancel Monday's meeting," Clarissa said through his phone's speaker. "Do you want me to reschedule?"

"Not yet," he said. "I didn't want to meet with him anyway. Tell him we'll connect later in the summer."

"Okay. Also, I just got word that the tickets for Senator Landry's reelection fund-raiser came through."

"Awesome," Damien said. "Put it on my calendar."

"Oh, and Kurt called. He wanted to know if you two were still on for lunch."

"Why didn't he text me?" Damien pulled his phone from his pocket, making sure nothing was wrong with it.

"He said he wanted to hear my sexy voice. Your brother is such a flirt."

Damien rolled his eyes. "I'll text him in a minute," Damien said. "Do you mind ordering chicken lo mein and the shrimp in garlic sauce from Five Happiness?"

"I'm here to grant your every wish," she said, eliciting another eye roll from Damien.

He quickly went through a few more emails before shutting down his computer. Just as he rose from his desk, Clarissa's voice came through the phone again.

"The *Gambit* is on hold," she said.

Damien stared at the red blinking light. He pressed the intercom for Clarissa. "Can you take a message?"

There was a beat of silence before he heard heels clopping and his door sprung open.

"Take the call," Clarissa said. "You do not turn down a call from the *Gambit*."

Damien cursed his decision to have a less formal office environment as he picked up the phone. As he expected, the paper, which was one of the top entertainment news outlets in the city, wanted to interview him for what they were calling NOLA Notables. Damien had no doubt that this was a direct result of the Top Ten Eligible Bachelors article. It was as if the floodgates had

been opened. He was no longer seen as just a businessman in the city. He was now a "notable."

Damien wasn't sure how to handle this. In a way,
it was press—it was *good* press. And good press was
golden. But he wasn't sure how this type of press would
come across to potential investors. Would they see it as
good-natured fun, or would they see it as a reason not
to take him seriously?

He would have to figure out how to make this new
local fame of his work to his advantage, because it
wasn't going away anytime soon. Something in his gut
told him that having April on his arm, with her refined
taste and regal manner, was the way to go.

Damien only hoped that he was making the right
decision. He had too much riding on this to get things
wrong.

Damien wound his way down the parking garage's
spiral ramp, then headed straight for his brother's favorite Chinese restaurant in what was known as the Carrollton area. The hostess knew him by face, seeing as
Damien made a weekly appearance at the restaurant.
He'd been stopping in for takeout every Friday for the
past two years, ever since he returned to New Orleans.

He backed out onto Carrollton Avenue and made his
way across the city to Bayou St. John. Damien considered this area, which was part of New Orleans's Mid-
City neighborhood, as the gold standard when it came
to locations that had revitalized themselves following
Hurricane Katrina. The neighborhood, which was made
up of a collection of colorfully painted houses done in
the colonial and Italianate styles, along with a number of one-of-a-kind eateries and retail shops, was the

heart of New Orleans. Residents banded together and rebuilt their community into something that was even more spectacular than it had been prior to the storm.

The area had grown by leaps and bounds in the past couple of years. Millennials who had come to New Orleans to take advantage of its budding tech industry, small families who'd moved out of the suburbs, but who still wanted the sense of a close-knit community, had found their way to Mid-City.

And where the people came, commerce followed. New businesses continued to spring up, changing the landscape of the neighborhood. It was exactly what Damien had in mind for Alexander Quarters. He could turn that area into a viable part of New Orleans, too.

Damien pulled into the driveway of the single-story bungalow he'd purchased for his brother two years ago. Instead of taking the front steps up to the porch, he walked along the access ramp, inspecting the wood for warping. After a week of late-evening downpours, Damien wanted to make sure the rain hadn't affected Kurt's mode of getting into the house.

Thankfully, according to the meteorologist, the rains were done for the rest of this evening. It shouldn't hamper the affair on Julia Street tonight.

The front door opened and Kurt wheeled himself out.

"Hey, man, what's going on?" His brother, who was older than Damien by four years, greeted him with a huge smile.

"Nothing much," Damien answered. "Other than you hitting on my office manager, that is." Taking the hand his brother held out to him, he bent low for a one-armed hug.

"Hey, she's the one who flirts with me," Kurt said.

"Says you. Clarissa tells another story. And the problem is I wouldn't know who to believe out of the two of you."

Kurt put a hand to his chest. "That hurts."

Damien knocked him on the shoulder. "Let's get inside and eat this food before it gets cold."

"Did you bring extra fortune cookies?"

"Don't I always bring extra fortune cookies?"

"What's with the attitude? Did you also get an extra bug up your ass?"

Damien didn't bother answering that. He held the door open while Kurt backed into the house. As he watched the motorized chair roll ahead of him, Damien fought off the wave of anger that tried to overtake him whenever he was reminded of Kurt's condition.

His throat tightened with emotion as he remembered that call he'd received from one of Kurt's old buddies from the neighborhood, telling Damien that his brother had been shot while walking to the corner store. Shot, just as his dad—a former officer with the NOPD—had been back when Damien was in middle school. His father had been gunned down on the streets of the Ninth Ward while off duty.

He and Kurt had buried their mother only a year before Kurt's shooting, after an aneurysm burst in her head on her way from church. The thought of losing Kurt, too—of being completely alone—had brought Damien to his knees, right in the middle of his office in Houston.

Doctors said Kurt's survival could only be described as a miracle. The three bullets that struck him had missed his vital organs by millimeters. But he would be in that chair for the rest of his life.

Those streets had taken his father from him. His mother had fallen dead on the sidewalk. And his brother had been robbed of his ability to walk. Damien was sure he would never be able to forgive or get over the toll that neighborhood had taken on his family.

But a few months ago Damien ran across the listing for the vacant lot on the northern tip of the area, and he'd gotten the idea to change things for the better. Instead of being bitter, he would usher in a new era, revitalize the neighborhood, bring in a new crop of residents and businesses that would make it a safer place to live. That was the legacy the Alexanders would leave in the Lower Ninth Ward.

"So," Kurt said as he dished them both plates of fragrant Chinese food. "Should I bring up the bachelor thing, or will you?"

Damien groaned. "Don't," he said. "I figured if there was anywhere that I could get away from it, it would be here."

"You figured wrong," Kurt said with a laugh. "You know the only reason you were chosen is because you're more well-known than I am, right? If they knew of this Alexander brother, your ugly mug wouldn't be splashed across those pages."

"Your ego is as healthy as ever."

"I'm just saying." His brother laughed again. It was good to hear laughter in this house.

They dug into the food as if they didn't eat the same thing week after week. A few minutes passed before Damien said, "I was down on St. Claude yesterday."

Kurt's eyes widened with interests. "You? You haven't been down that way since Mama's funeral."

"It hasn't been that long," Damien argued, although

there was a good chance his brother was right. "Have I told you about the youth program April Knight works with? It's called A Fresh Start."

"Yeah, I know about it. They're building some kind of community coffee shop. I saw it online."

"It opened already," Damien said. "I went out there to visit it and, you know, just to see how things are going."

"Hmm," Kurt said.

"What's the 'hmm' about?"

Kurt shook his head.

Damien could sense that all-knowing Obi-Wan Kenobi vibe resonating from him. He set his fork down and lifted his hand. "What, Kurt? Just spit it out."

"Nothing. It's just that I'm assuming you saw April while you were there?"

Damien's brow furrowed at the suggestion in Kurt's tone. "Yeah, so?"

"Oh, come on," his brother said. "You still playing that denial game where April is concerned?"

"Don't start this again." Damien stood and walked over to the shelf so he could scoop more lo mein onto his plate. "April and I have always been just friends. You know that."

"You're an idiot."

"Because I'm friends with April?"

"Because you're blind when it comes to April," Kurt countered.

Showed how much his brother knew. Not only was Damien *not* blind to her, but he'd had a helluva time getting the image of her standing in front of the class instructing her students out of his mind. There was something in the joy on her face that called to him. He tried to ignore it, but it wasn't easy.

"I only want lunch today," Damien said. "Advice from the Love Doctor is not necessary."

"In addition to being smart and talented, April is a knockout. I saw this concert she performed on PBS not too long ago—"

"Since when do you watch PBS?"

"Shut up."

"Comeback of the year." Damien snorted.

"All I'm saying," his brother continued, "is that you're stupid to just leave April out there for another guy to snatch up."

Damien shoveled another forkful of lo mein into his mouth to give him an excuse not to speak. Because, honestly, he didn't know how to respond to his brother's statement.

It's not as if he needed Kurt to tell him that April was beautiful, especially after seeing her yesterday. He had eyes. And when it came to spotting a beautiful woman, they worked extremely well.

And it wasn't as if Damien hadn't allowed that particular scenario to play in his mind in years past, either. Hell, how could he not? He'd known April since their sophomore year of high school. Back in those days his horny teenaged mind had imagined nearly every non-blood-related female he came in contact with in a compromising position. But he'd felt guilty thinking about April in those terms. She was his friend. She'd reached out to him out of the kindness of that big heart to tutor him. She didn't deserve to be thrust into a starring role in his wet dreams.

So Damien had tamed those wild thoughts when it came to April. Once they graduated from high school it became a bit easier. They talked through phone and email throughout college, with her still helping him with his schoolwork, even though hundreds of miles had separated them. But once they were both done with school and on to their careers, the phone calls had become less frequent.

Damien had made sure he attended her performances whenever she was in Houston, and he'd even caught a few outside Texas, both in LA and in DC a few years back when she'd performed for the president. But those encounters had been far too infrequent over the years.

He was damn lucky April was still single and able to help him out with these social events this summer.

"Damien? Damien!"

"Huh? What?" Damien shot out of his chair and raced over to Kurt. "Is something wrong?"

"Other than the fact that I've been calling your name for a solid minute?" His brother shook his head. "I hope you don't space out on your clients like that."

Damien sucked in a breath to try to calm his heart's rapid beating. Running a hand down his face, he blew out a relieved sigh.

"I'm sorry," he said. "I just have a lot on my mind these days."

"Fending off all the women who want to take away your bachelor status?"

Damien slanted him a look. It would have silenced most people. It only made Kurt laugh out loud.

"Now that you're done making fun of me, I'll go back to the office," Damien said. "I've got this thing tonight in the Warehouse District and I need to get some work done before it starts."

He began cleaning up the food, but Kurt rolled up next to him and pulled his hand away.

"I've got this," Kurt said.

"I'm just putting the leftovers away for you."

"I can do that myself."

Damien lifted both hands in surrender. He wasn't up for this argument today. God knew they'd had it more times than he could count. His brother was nothing if not independent, and he had no problem chewing Damien out if he tried to step in where he wasn't needed.

"Have at it," Damien said. "I need to get back anyway."

He headed for the door, Kurt following behind.

Once out on the porch, Damien turned back to his brother. "Remember, the guy from that mechanical-chair company is coming on Thursday to get you fitted and take measurements of the house."

"I told you already that I'm not getting that new chair if it means renovating the house," Kurt said.

"And I told you that I don't give a damn what you say, not when it comes to this."

"You forgetting who the oldest is?" his brother asked.

"We're going by tallest on this one. That new chair can elevate you to a standing position, so if you had it, you'd win the argument. But since you don't, I win. The sales rep comes on Thursday. I'll try to get here before he does."

"Still a little pain in the ass," Kurt said.

"It's in the 'baby of the family' job description."

Kurt laughed. "Thanks for lunch."

"Always." Damien leaned over and gave him a hug. "Same time, same meal next week."

"Ugh, I hate this part. I always mess up on it."

April rounded the music stand and stood next to Linsey Turner, who was currently staring at the cello in her hands as though she wanted to heave the huge instrument across the room. Which was why April quickly interceded. Instruments were hard to come by for A Fresh Start, so April did everything she could to preserve the few they had.

"Don't get frustrated," she told the teen. "It'll only cause you to lose your concentration. You know this piece. You don't need this." She moved the music stand out of the way. "Now, close your eyes and concentrate on the notes. Remember what I said before—allow yourself to feel the music. Now start from the top."

April studied the teen's face as her eyelids fell closed and she gently drew the bow across the taut strings. She could see Linsey tense as she came upon the second measure.

"Relax," April encouraged. "Don't rush it."

The fingers that gently plucked the strings eased, and the harmonious notes of Bach's Second Concerto drifted through the room. A huge smile drew across April's lips.

"There you go," she said. "Perfect."

"Not perfect," Linsey said, "but close. You'd better watch out. I'm coming for your job."

"You just try, Ms. Smarty-Pants," April said with a laugh. "I can always use an assistant. Keep playing like this and I'll make you one."

"Promise?"

"Maybe," April said, warming to the idea. "I've been thinking about adding a beginner's course for the younger kids. If you keep it up, I think you may get to a level where you can teach them the basics."

"Really?" Linsey's eyes grew wide. "That would be awesome."

The mixture of excitement and awe in the young girl's face pretty much sealed the deal for April. It had taken her a while to get Linsey to open up to her. Even though the kids here appreciated them—they wouldn't attend A Fresh Start if they didn't—a lot of them still looked at the adults as big, bad authority figures who should be avoided at all cost. Breaking through that barrier wasn't always easy, but April refused to give up the fight.

"I need to get home," Linsey said as she packed up her backpack. "I told my mom I'd cook dinner tonight so she could go wedding dress shopping with my aunt Theresa." The fourteen-year-old rolled her eyes.

"What's with the look?" April asked.

"The wedding will probably be off by next week," Linsey said. "This is the third time they've gone wedding dress shopping this year. Aunt Theresa always gets cold feet."

Linsey waved as she exited the room. April picked up scattered pages of sheet music, her spirits light as she remembered how well her pupils had performed today. None were as talented as Linsey—the girl had a special gift when it came to picking up musical notes—but, as a whole, her most advanced class was an extremely special group. She'd taken a set of kids who had no interest whatsoever in classical music and turned them into a bunch of budding protégés. It wasn't all that strange to hear someone humming Vivaldi or Beethoven down the halls of A Fresh Start. That was something she could be proud of.

This was her second year with this particular group

of students. They were a little rusty, but not much. April had been thrilled to learn that some of them had met throughout the school year, using instruments they'd purchased at a thrift store, and practicing so that they could keep up their skills. How much more amazing would they be if A Fresh Start became a year-round program?

"It's going to happen," April said. "You're going to make this happen."

April felt her phone buzz in her pocket. She pulled it out to find a text message from Damien.

I'll be there to pick you up at 7 p.m. Remember to wear blue.

A nauseating mixture of anxiety and anticipation swirled around in her stomach, making her queasy. There was still time to get out of this. Sure, she and Damien had gone out for dinner before, but that was as friends. Other than the pity date he'd treated her to for their senior prom, this would be her first time going out with him on an actual date.

"It's not a real date," April reminded herself.

But they were pretending that it was a real date, so it was starting to feel that way. She didn't need her silly little mind going places that it absolutely should not go.

She could handle this. She and Damien had made a fair bargain. She was going to uphold her end of it, because she sure wanted him to uphold his end.

April texted back: See you at seven.

She added her address because in the two years since she'd been in her house, Damien had never once come over. Of course, she had not been to his home, either. They really sucked at this friendship thing.

It was disappointing, because at one time they'd been so close that it was nothing to have Damien come over to her parents' place for dinner, or vice versa. They should both feel ashamed for allowing their friendship to grow apart as much as it had.

April put away the instruments and locked them in the storage closet. On her way out, she asked the janitor to pay special attention to the floors behind the counter in the new coffee shop. The kids were responsible for keeping their workplace clean, but it was apparent to April that their version of clean was vastly different from hers.

She slipped behind the wheel of her Nissan Altima and headed down St. Claude Avenue.

When she'd returned to New Orleans a couple of years ago, April decided to move to the Bywater neighborhood. The area, which was just west of the Lower Ninth Ward and within walking distance of the French Quarter, had seen a complete overhaul following Hurricane Katrina.

April had been living out of state for a few years before Katrina hit, but all of her family had still lived in New Orleans, with two of her brothers in the Lower Ninth Ward at the time. The breach of the Industrial Canal took care of that. Her childhood home was completely destroyed, along with the homes her older brothers Nicholas and Savion had both bought. The eldest, Jason, had moved to another part of the city, which was also inundated with floodwater. At one point they were all living in different parts of the country.

Her three brothers eventually returned to the New

Orleans area, but her parents had decided they were done with hurricanes. They moved to Albuquerque, finding the heat easier to deal with than killer storms.

There were a number of neighborhoods that had come back stronger than ever following Katrina, which made April even more disheartened when she thought about the Ninth Ward. It had been one of the hardest hit and its recovery had been one of the slowest.

But longtime residents were looking to change that. After government agencies proved to be unreliable, the people here had taken matters into their own hands. Slowly but surely, they were rebuilding their community. More and more projects were launching every month. Soon, the Ninth Ward would be among those post-Katrina success stories.

When April arrived home, she immediately pulled out the leftover Italian food she had from last night and nuked it in the microwave. She'd skipped lunch, and she wasn't sure what kind of food would be available at this street fair they were going to.

After kicking off her shoes and throwing on a robe, she picked up her iPad and finally checked her emails, something else she hadn't had a chance to do yet. The first email to catch her eye was one from her agent, Carlos, with the subject line "BOSTON and PHILLY."

If April didn't know better she would have thought the instant, erratic pounding of her heart signaled an impending heart attack. But she ate right and exercised regularly; she knew her heart was in pristine condition. To a philharmonic musician, the words *Boston* and *Philly* had a particular meaning.

But this couldn't mean *that*, could it?

After years of traveling the globe with various music

companies, April was perfectly content with the type of work she did now. The only time she traveled was to perform the occasional movie score, but that required no more than a week or two away from home. She'd told Carlos that she was not interested in playing with any live orchestras.

Unless it was in Boston or Philadelphia.

But these two companies were two of the hardest to get on with, even for someone with a résumé like the one April boasted.

She opened Carlos's email and her breathing escalated. He had indeed been in talks with the conductors of the Boston Pops and Philadelphia Philharmonic Orchestra. Of course, "in talks" didn't equate to an actual audition, but it was enough to get April's blood racing.

However, the excitement soon dissipated, and a boatload of anxiety settled in its place.

What about her kids at A Fresh Start?

If she left to join another orchestra, would the music program die? Would all those kids who were blossoming more and more every day lose their passion for it, and instead turn to more unsavory activities?

When LaDonna first approached her about volunteering at A Fresh Start, April had warned her that it would only be temporary. She'd just moved back to New Orleans, and was planning to use her newly purchased house solely as a home base. The nature of her work called for her to be flexible.

But as she'd started to do more work that could be done remotely, the idea of all those long hours on the road, sleeping in different hotels every night and eating packaged airport food had lost what little appeal it once held. And the more time she spent at A Fresh

Start, seeing the actual difference she was making in the lives of kids from her old neighborhood, the more she wanted to stay and do even more to bring about change in the Ninth Ward.

But the Boston Pops?

There was not a cellist worth her salt who would ever turn down the chance to play with the Boston Pops.

But it wasn't a done deal. Not by a long shot.

Goodness, it wasn't even an audition. Who knew what, if anything, would come of these "talks" between Carlos and the conductors in Boston and Philly? She could be getting herself all worked up for nothing.

Instead, April needed to turn her focus to the very real issues currently on her plate, specifically the matter of the date she would be late for if she didn't start getting ready.

And just like that, her heart started that wild, erratic beating again. She had a feeling she would experience that a lot throughout the rest of the night. Spending this time with Damien, pretending to be his girlfriend, was sure to give her heart a workout.

Chapter 4

Damien adjusted his car vents so that the air hit him directly in the face. The brief rainstorm that had popped up out of nowhere had passed, but the heat and humidity it left behind made him feel as if he would suffocate. He had no one to blame but himself. He'd been back in south Louisiana long enough to have realized that wearing a suit jacket—even a linen one—this time of the year was akin to torture. There was no way in hell he would spend the night in this thing. It was going in his trunk.

He found a parking spot across the street from April's home in Bywater. Its wooden clapboards were painted lilac. Not a surprise. He remembered it was her favorite color. What *was* a surprise was the playful feel of the place. It was accented with white shutters and gingerbread trim. The small, neatly kept front yard had several colorful bird feeders, and a metal wind chime hung from the eaves above the front porch.

He wouldn't have pegged April as one for whimsy, but what did he know? He hadn't pegged her as someone who would be willing to lie on a grant application, either. That she had even suggested it had shocked the hell out of him yesterday. The April he knew would never even consider doing something like that.

Then again, the April he knew had always been willing to do whatever she could to help those in need.

Like him.

A small smile tickled the corners of Damien's lips as he recalled the way she'd approached him all those years ago, back when they were in high school. Because they lived on opposite sides of the Lower Ninth Ward, they had attended different elementary and middle schools. At the time, the only thing Damien knew about her was her name. To him, April was simply the quiet girl who never really said anything in class unless it was to answer a question from the teacher—something she did on a regular basis. She didn't socialize much with the other students.

Except for that day when she'd stopped him on his way out of Mrs. Blanchard's English class and offered to tutor him. Damien had responded by being a defensive little shit, because, well, that's just the kind of kid he'd been back then. The fact that she'd approached him in front of several of their classmates, who snickered at her offer, only made things worse.

Damien was sure all he had to do was growl in her direction to send her running, but he soon learned that when April Knight decided to champion a cause, she didn't scare easily. She'd persisted, standing next to his table in the lunchroom while his friends looked on in curiosity, catching him in the halls. She would slip bits of paper with study suggestions scrawled on them through the slits in his locker, along with her email address in case he wanted to talk it over.

After several weeks of Damien applying those study methods she'd suggested, April accosted him in the hallway, and told him that she believed he could do so much better if he stopped being such a stubborn fathead and allowed her to help him. That the quiet slip of a girl called him a fathead to his face had shocked him, but not nearly as much as hearing her say that she believed in him.

That moment in the crowded hallway of Carver High School had been a turning point. Damien would forever be grateful for her tenacity. She'd turned his life around by extending that helping hand. She'd changed his perspective. Once he started working with April, he wanted to do better—be better. For her.

He'd discovered that it was still the case today. He wanted April to be proud of the kind of man he'd become. He hadn't realized just how much her approval still influenced him.

Damien walked up to her small porch, which, in addition to the wind chime, had several potted ivy plants in hanging baskets. Their long vines cascaded down, creating a curtain that shaded portions of the porch. He approached the door and rang the doorbell, and heard April's muffled voice just on the other side.

The door opened and Damien felt as if he'd been struck in the chest.

She was stunning. She wore an airy sundress with thin straps and a hem that looked as if it was ripped apart in strips. The material had swirls of dark blue over a lighter blue backdrop, with tiny dots of silver sprinkled throughout.

"You look amazing," Damien said.

"Thank you," she replied. Was that a blush he saw climbing up her cheeks, or had she been out in the heat, too? Later, when he had time to process the thoughts and feelings swirling in his brain, he would figure out why the thought of putting a blush on her face made him feel so damn good.

April moved aside so he could enter.

"Can you give me a couple of minutes? You're early. I haven't finished getting ready."

Damien would beg to differ. He didn't see a single thing on her that looked as if it needed fixing in any way.

"There's juice and soda in the fridge if you want any," she said. "There may be a beer in there, too."

Parched from his sweltering ride over, Damien helped himself to a bottled water from her refrigerator, then said in a voice loud enough to carry to the back of the house where she'd gone off to, "If you were considering bringing a light sweater or something, forget it. It's brutal out there."

A couple of moments passed before April entered the kitchen, fixing an earring to her ear. "Oh, I know better than to worry with a cover-up," April said. "We're not getting under eighty degrees for the next few months. All my sweaters are put away until October."

"How long did it take you to readjust to this south Louisiana heat?" Damien asked.

She twisted up a corner of her mouth. "Not as long as I thought. I did that stint in Brazil, remember? That was even hotter than New Orleans for a huge portion of the time. But you were in Houston. It's not that different."

Setting his backside against the edge of the counter, Damien peered at her as he tipped his head back to take a sip of water. "It isn't always as humid there." He paused for a beat before continuing. "I know we came back to New Orleans around the same time, but I have to admit that it still surprises me that you chose to settle down here."

Her forehead dipped in a confused crease. "Why's that?"

"With all the places you've visited and lived over the years, I would have thought you'd end up in New York, or San Francisco, or even Paris."

April shrugged. "I love all those cities, but they all have one thing that's missing," she said. "They're not home. *This* is home. I think I made the right decision."

"So do I," Damien said. He gestured around the kitchen. "Although, I must say that I was a bit thrown by this particular house."

"You don't like my house?" Her frown was as adorable as the rest of her.

"I love your house. It's just…not what I expected," Damien said. He pushed away from the counter and walked over to where she stood, just next to the stove. "I've discovered several unexpected things about you over the last couple of days."

"Such as?" she asked in a voice that hovered just above a whisper. It felt as if the oxygen in the kitchen had all but evaporated.

"Such as this little bargain you forced me to agree to," Damien said.

"Forced?"

"Made damn near impossible to reject," Damien amended. He took another step closer. "The April Knight I used to know wouldn't have had the guts to make the kind of demand you made yesterday."

"I'm not the quiet girl you used to know," she said.

Electricity sizzled between them. Damien experienced the same jolt he'd felt when she visited his office. It made his skin feel tight, caused the air in his lungs to evaporate.

He took another step toward her, but then she broke eye contact, slipping away from the counter and walking over to the opposite side of the kitchen. She moved a paper towel holder a few inches to the right and brushed invisible dirt from the counter.

"So, this thing that we're going to tonight, what exactly am I supposed to do?"

Damien didn't answer right away. He continued to stare at her, debating whether to give voice to the moment that had just passed between them, or ignore it and pretend it didn't happen. As he considered the hours ahead of them, and how he needed April to be as comfortable as possible so that she could help him woo New Orleans's elite, he decided to go with ignoring it. There was too much riding on the outcome of the various events he had lined up to risk spooking April.

Damien braced his feet apart and crossed his arms over his chest.

"A week ago I would have said that I wanted you there just so I wouldn't look like the guy who couldn't get a date," he answered. "But after this thing with that magazine, I need you to run interference for me. I've been approached by a few...how do I say it? Overeager females."

"So I'm the designated cock blocker?"

A sharp laugh shot out of his mouth.

"April Knight," Damien said in an admonishing tone. "Where'd you learn such language?"

The grin that pulled at the edges of her lips was so damn cute Damien wanted to snap her picture so that he could revisit it whenever he needed a pick-me-up.

"Don't tell my brothers," she said.

"Oh, I would love to see the looks on the Knight brothers' faces if they heard what their innocent little sister just said."

The grin that slid across her mouth this time was decidedly wicked. "You know, I'm not as innocent as I look."

The words, spoken in that hushed, seductive tone, drizzled down Damien's spine like warm nectar. They were tiptoeing into dangerous territory here. This was April, for goodness' sake. He needed to bring them back to a safer playing field.

"So, about tonight," Damien said.

April cleared her throat and moved the paper towel holder back to where it had originally sat. "Yes. Tonight," she said.

"It's a bit like White Linen Night that takes place in August. Several of the art galleries along Julia Street will have their doors open to the public. All participating artists are donating a portion of their profits from tonight to the local charities that support autism research. Ten of the city's top restaurants will have booths set up on the sidewalk, selling refreshments."

"And how will this help *your* particular cause?"

"The McGowan Group is one of the event's main

sponsors. They're the perfect fit for this special project I'm working on."

"You mind sharing exactly what this special project is?" April asked.

"I thought I told you?"

"No, you haven't. You do realize that before you walked into A Fresh Start the other day, I hadn't seen you since Christmas, right?"

Damien nodded. He did realize that. And he felt awful about it.

"I'm as much to blame as you are," April said, as if she'd read his thoughts. A wan smile lifted the corner of her mouth. "Your number is saved in my contact list. I could just as easily call you. We need to make more of an effort to stay in touch, especially now that we're both living back home."

"Well, now that we're going to be spending so much time together this summer, it won't take as much effort. In a few weeks you'll probably be hiding from me."

Her eyes shone with a flash of raw heat. "I doubt that," she said.

There it was again. That current of electricity. It sparked between them, filling the small kitchen with an energy he couldn't describe.

"So, your project?" April asked.

"Uh, yeah, the project," Damien said. When was the last time he'd found himself feeling so flustered? "I want to build a residential complex," he said.

Her eyes blinked several times, her head tilting to the side in confusion. "In the Ninth Ward?"

"Yes. On the land I just bought. I want to help bring residents back by providing housing."

"That's wonderful, Damien." April's face softened

and he felt as if he'd just been handed the entire world. "I had no idea that's what you were doing."

Pride swelled within his chest.

It was the look that was in her eyes right that second that had compelled him to want to be a better person. The look that said that he'd made her happy, that he'd given her a reason to be proud of him. That look used to fuel nearly everything he did back when he was in high school.

One would think that making his mother proud would be the thing that kept him going, but after his dad died, his mother had always been too busy to pay much attention to what he was doing.

It was an uneasy truth, but a truth nonetheless. A single mother working two jobs to supplement the meager survivor's benefits they received following his dad's off-duty murder didn't have time to dole out praise for each and every little achievement. As long as he and Kurt came home every night and didn't wind up in jail or the morgue, his mother was happy.

April was the person Damien wanted to impress. April was the one who was there to give him high fives when he aced a test, or got good marks on term papers.

And just as it had been back in those days at Carver High School, Damien wanted to impress her now.

He shrugged, as if putting that smile on her face wasn't a big deal. "I figured I'm in the perfect position to do it," he said.

"You're also the perfect *person* to do it," April replied. "Residents are far more likely to support this development if it's someone from the neighborhood who's driving it."

"I can't do it alone, though," Damien said. "Which

is why I need investors. I researched potential partners, and the McGowan Group is by far the best match for what I have in mind. I just need to convince them that they want to work with me."

"You're pretty good at convincing people to bend to your will when you put your mind to it," she said. "I don't think you'll have a problem winning them over."

"I like your confidence in me."

She took his hands and clasped them between her own. "I mean it, Damien. You can do this."

The smile in her eyes did more for him than any of those motivational posters his old boss used to plaster around the office.

"Thanks for the vote of confidence," he said.

"Anytime and every time. Now, let's go," April said. She gave his hands a light squeeze. "I'm ready to see you in action."

By the time they arrived in the Warehouse District, the street parking was completely taken up. Damien pulled into a covered garage two blocks from Julia Street and started for the area known to locals as Gallery Row.

A three-block stretch of Julia had been blocked off to traffic. Lights were strung from one side of the street to the other, the pale blue bulbs casting an ethereal hue over the crowd of sharply dressed patrons. White-jacketed waiters freely handed out champagne, courtesy of the event's corporate sponsors. The McGowan Group's logo—the letter *M* encased in a square—adorned the champagne bottles and paper napkins.

Conversation and laughter lit up the air, which shouldn't have been a surprise to anyone in attendance. This was

New Orleans, after all. And if there was one thing the Big Easy knew how to do, it was throw a party.

Walking a step ahead of him, though still holding on to his hand, April looked at Damien over her nearly bare shoulder. Her smooth skin had already developed a slight sheen from the humidity hanging heavily in the air.

"Are you ready to mingle?" she asked.

Damien nodded. "Let's do this."

He wasn't sure what he'd expected, but he sure as hell hadn't anticipated that April would have just about everyone eating out the palm of her hand within the first twenty minutes. Yet he shouldn't be surprised. She'd spent over a decade hobnobbing with dignitaries, celebrities and wealthy symphony buffs. She knew how to charm this type of crowd.

The two of them entered a gallery that, according to the platinum plate just outside the door, displayed modern mixed-media art. Damien had never been one for staring at a piece of artwork and dissecting its meaning. If something looked like bits of construction paper glued together by a four-year-old, then that's what he was going to call it. However, in her life of world travels and mingling with the rich and cultured, April had apparently learned how to tell the junk from the…well… as far as he was concerned, bigger junk.

Several fellow gallery-goers gathered around them to discuss the quality of the various works, expounding on the richness and passion. Damien simply nodded and smiled while April worked her magic. She was brilliant.

They dipped in and out of several galleries. Just as he'd anticipated, a number of people brought up the magazine article. Several of the women gave April long, curious looks, but none remarked on the fact that one of the city's top bachelors had a date on his arm.

He and April visited five galleries before Damien finally spotted Michael Berger, one of the managing partners of the McGowan Group.

"That's him," Damien said. He tipped the champagne flute he'd grabbed from a passing waiter a few minutes ago toward the tall gentleman with salt-and-pepper hair. "That's the one I'm here to see."

"The one wearing the tie with Van Gogh's *Starry Night* on it?" April asked.

"I have no idea what you're talking about," Damien said.

With an exasperated sigh, she said, "The tall one standing next to the redhead?"

"Yes," he answered. "I've met him a couple of times, but it's been a few months."

"Okay," April said. "Let's go."

They started for Berger, but they were stopped just a few feet away from him by a reporter with a cameraman. Damien recognized the local news station's logo on the side of the camera.

She stuck her hand out. "Hi, I'm Rebecca James from Channel 9. How lucky to run into you here, Mr. Alexander. I hope you don't mind the ambush, but I'd love to get some live comments from you."

"Actually, I—"

The reporter turned and nodded at the cameraman, and suddenly the camera's shining light blinded Damien.

"Here we are at Art for Autism," the tall brunette with the Colgate smile said into the camera. "And it should come as no surprise to see local entrepreneur

Damien Alexander here. We all know that this worthy cause is worth patronizing, but I think what's on the minds of most in the Crescent City is what it feels like to be named one of the city's top eligible bachelors. So, Damien?"

At first, April was unsure of what to do. Damien's deer-in-the-headlights expression was so foreign to anything she'd ever witnessed from him that it completely caught her off guard. But she quickly recovered. She recognized the tension that had slowly begun to rise in him by the way the smooth skin stretching over his defined cheekbones grew taut.

Pasting on an overly bright smile, April stepped in between Damien and the reporter.

"Actually," she started, "I think Mr. Alexander would rather discuss why it meant so much for both of us to attend this wonderful event on behalf of children with autism."

"Oh, of course," the reporter said. "But we all know that the viewers out there would love a word from him about being named one of the city's best catches."

"He finds it flattering," April answered for him. "Now, about Art for Autism."

Taking the reporter by the hand, she led her to the other side of the gallery, pulling out all the trite responses that reporters expect at an event such as this one. April looked back at Damien and gave him a subtle nod toward Michael Berger.

As she continued with the rambling reporter, she watched him approach the multimillionaire who'd made such an impact on the city since his arrival several years ago. April itched to be involved in the conversation. She wasn't sure why it had just occurred to her that she and Damien could pull double duty on this quest he had to woo the city's elite. She didn't want to step on his toes by taking anything away from his search to find investors, but there were some über-rich people floating through the various galleries tonight; surely they could afford to send some of that wealth A Fresh Start's way.

April was able to shake the reporter after telling her that Damien was taking the bachelor thing all in good fun. She quickly returned to his side…just as Berger was leaving.

"Thank you for that," Damien told her. "It wasn't the type of interference I thought you'd have to run, but you did a bang-up job all the same."

"That's my part of the deal, isn't it?" April said. "Now, how did it go with Berger?"

He hunched his shoulders. "Okay, I guess. I didn't hit him with the hard sale or anything. I just told him that I'd love to work with the McGowan Group on a project someday. Stroked his ego a bit, told him how impressed I am with all the ventures they've started here in New Orleans. I think it went well."

"Look at you," April said, nudging him with her shoulder. "When did you learn how to schmooze?"

"It's a part of the job," he said with a laugh. "And as for your job tonight, you are going above and beyond."

"How so?"

"Because you're making me look good. I don't know a damn thing about art. If not for you, I'd have looked like an idiot tonight."

"No, you wouldn't. You can BS your way through anything, Damien. I discovered that the day you convinced Mr. Pendleton to let you out of taking the chemistry final because you believed the periodic table was against your religion."

His head kicked back with his laugh. "That was a pretty sweet moment."

"It was epic." April laughed along with him. "When you put your mind to it, you can do just about anything. I suspect you would have done just fine without me."

"But it wouldn't have been nearly as enjoyable," he said. His eyes glittered with mischief, but also with just enough heat to make April suck in a breath.

When he leaned forward, she became light-headed.

But he didn't go near her mouth, which was exactly where her overly active imagination had pictured him heading. Instead, he whispered in her ear, "Thank you for being by my side tonight. And for having so much knowledge about art in that brain of yours."

April put a lid on the can of wishful thinking that had her imagining Damien kissing her, and reminded herself exactly why she was here and what was expected of her. And of him.

"As you may recall," she said, "this all comes at a price. I expect to see you at A Fresh Start bright and early tomorrow. It'll be just an introduction, but once you're done with tomorrow's class we'll work on a more formal syllabus."

A pained look flashed across Damien's face.

"I guess there's no way for me to back out of the deal now, is there?"

April hooked a thumb over her shoulder. "You want me to go find Rebecca James? I'm sure she and her cameraman would still love to speak to you, Mr. Top Ten Bachelor."

"I'll be at the center tomorrow. You're ruthless, by

the way," Damien said, taking her by the hand and leading her out of the gallery.

"You'd better remember that," April told him.

The crowds filling the street had started to thin, making it easier to navigate from gallery to gallery, and from food booth to food booth. April laughed herself into a coughing fit when Damien bit into a shrimp creole–stuffed beignet and sent all the filling flying out the opposite end of the bread.

A brass jazz band started to play, and Damien held a hand out to her.

April shook her head. "I don't think so," she said.

"Hey, aren't you the musician here?"

"And when does being a musician equal being a dancer?"

"Hmm," Damien murmured. He shoved his hands in his pockets and looked up at the sky. "I can recall coaxing you onto the dance floor at the senior prom and you shocking everybody with your dance moves."

April couldn't help the huge smile that formed on her face. "Fine, I used to watch music videos and practice in my room. But that was a long time ago," she added. She could feel the blush climbing up her cheeks. "I don't dance anymore."

Damien held his hand out again.

"Please?" he said. He had the nerve to sic the puppy dog eyes on her. He was not playing fair at all. "Just this once?" he added.

"God, you're needy," she groused.

He barked out another laugh as April reluctantly allowed him to pull her out into the middle of the street, where dozens of other revelers dressed in their finery danced to the brass band. Second lining, as it was known, was a New Orleans tradition. It didn't matter if you were hosting a run-of-the-mill house party or a fancy shindig like the one they were attending tonight; no celebration in the Big Easy was complete until partygoers marched the second line.

With her arm hooked in the crook of Damien's, April continued down the street, waving the handkerchief he'd handed her in the air and high-stepping along with the trail of revelers. April could feel the heat from Damien's body all along her side where they occasionally touched. It ignited dozens of tingling sensations, sending them scattering across her skin.

She didn't want to feel this way, dammit! She'd put it in her head to fight these feelings with everything she had.

But they were too hard to fight.

So, instead, April allowed the fantasy to play out in her mind. She let herself pretend that she wasn't here as Damien's pretend girlfriend, but as the real thing. She didn't care if it made her seem like the dreamer she'd been back in high school, when he'd treated her kindly because she tutored him, and had taken her to the prom because no one else asked her. Maybe she was foolish to let herself go there, but she was going to indulge in this fantasy while she had the chance.

"Are you ready to head home?" Damien asked once the brass band brought their energetic play to a close.

"I guess—" April stopped midsentence, unable to halt the huge yawn that broke free. "So," she finished. "Does that answer your question?"

"Loud and clear," he said with another laugh.

Taking her by the hand, they returned to Damien's sleek black Mercedes. And, as April had expected, by the time they arrived back to her neighborhood there was no street parking anywhere near her house.

"What the heck's going on here?" Damien asked as he inched the car down the street.

"It's the Frenchmen Art Market, along with people going to all the new bars that have opened up in the Faubourg Marigny."

"But the Marigny is blocks away," he said.

"A lot of people hang out there, especially on the nights when they hold the art market. It gets worse every single week," April said. "But how can I complain when it's supporting artists?"

Damien looked at her with a knowing grin. "Still championing the little guy, huh?"

"Of course," she said. "Especially struggling artists. I understand their plight."

He was quiet for a moment, then asked, "You're not still struggling, are you? I mean financially."

"No," April said. "You know I'm not."

"Well, it's not as if we discuss finances," he said. "I just want to make sure you're okay. I know you do some kind of freelance thing, but I don't know how that work is going."

"That work is going fabulously," April said. "Just last week I had to turn down work on a score for a Hollywood film, because I just have too much work coming my way."

"Did they want you to fly to LA?"

"They did for this particular project, but usually I work remotely from a recording studio at the University of New Orleans. They rent out the space when it isn't being used."

"Sounds pretty convenient."

"You gotta love technology," April said. She looked over at him with a smile. "It's adorable that you would worry, but honestly, I'm in the best financial shape that I've ever been in. The work is good, and the money is good. I actually started doing some shows around town, too."

Damien's head swung her way. "Really? Where?"

"The Gravier Street Social Club. They host small concerts. I played one a few weeks ago, and agreed to get on their schedule for a few more."

"The great April Knight is back behind the cello? Nice."

She rolled her eyes, but couldn't hold in a snicker.

When they drove past her house a third time, April said, "You can just drop me off here and I'll walk home."

"I'm not just dropping you off. I don't care how comfortable you are in your neighborhood," Damien said.

"You do realize that I often walk home alone, don't you?"

"Not when I'm around."

He finally pulled into a spot three blocks from her house and cut the engine.

"This is ridiculous," April said, but he was already out of the car and coming over to her side. He opened her door and held his hand out to her.

"Let me show you the proper gentleman I've become. In case you've forgotten, I wasn't always this way."

"How could I forget?" April said with a laugh.

She remembered that afternoon well. She went off on Damien when he stood there waiting for her to open the door to study hall, even though she had just as many books in her arms as he did.

"God, but you were a Neanderthal back then," April said, taking his hand and allowing him to help her out of the car.

Damien nodded in agreement. "Practically spoke in grunts. Do you remember *April's Guide to Proper Etiquette*?"

April burst out laughing as she recalled that pretentious purple binder she'd put together for him back when he was preparing for college interviews.

"You carried that thing around for a month."

"I wanted to do well when I met with college recruiters, and because of you, I did. You have to admit that your student has come a long way." He took her hand and placed it in the crook of his elbow.

"Yes, you have," April said.

As they walked along the sidewalk, they discussed what he talked about with Berger and what Damien thought his chances were of convincing the businessman to join him.

"It was hard to gauge his interest, but I expected that would be the case. I've heard that he has a good poker face."

"Well, maybe he— Oh!" April felt herself going down, a victim of the crack in the sidewalk that she normally avoided on her morning jog. Before she could slam face-first into the pavement, a set of strong arms grasped her, muscled forearms settling underneath her breasts.

Air rushed out of her lungs and the heat that infused her body was powerful enough to scorch. It raced along her skin, slamming into her bloodstream.

"Are you okay?" Damien asked.

April looked up over her shoulder and suddenly

couldn't breathe. The sight of his handsome face so close to hers robbed her of her ability to speak. Yet, even if her muddled brain could think of words to say, April doubted her voice would cooperate. Instead, she nodded as she allowed Damien to lift her up.

He righted her, but he didn't let go of her. He turned her around, his arms never leaving her waist.

April finally released a breath. She could feel herself getting light-headed, though she wasn't sure if it was due to the lack of air in her lungs or the feel of Damien's solid strength still surrounding her.

"Are you sure you're okay?" His voice was deeper than it had been just a moment ago.

"Yes," April said, finally finding her voice. "That sidewalk… The neighborhood association has been after the city to fix it."

She retreated from his hold. April was certain she'd never been more reluctant to do anything in her life.

Damien reached for her hand and entwined his fingers with hers. He pulled her closer and whispered against her temple, "I'm happy they haven't gotten around to it yet."

A shudder cascaded down her spine.

"Don't tell my neighbors," April whispered, "but so am I."

Damien's deep, sexy chuckle did nothing to aid in her quest to get these tingles under control. They continued their stroll toward her house. When he walked her up to the porch, April started to ask him if he wanted to come inside, but before she could put voice to the words, Damien asked, "So, what time should I be there tomorrow?"

Disappointment assaulted her, but April sucked it up

and managed to answer, "Nine o'clock. The kids usually get in around nine thirty."

"Okay." He nodded, a small smile on his lips. "I'll see you then. Thanks for being awesome tonight."

"I'm just holding up my end of the bargain," April said. Then she slipped into the house and closed the door behind her.

She could hardly wait to go to bed. She was bound to have some seriously good dreams tonight.

Chapter 5

As he lifted his leather messenger bag from his trunk, Damien couldn't shake the anxiety pulsing through his bloodstream. He didn't want to be here. He wouldn't admit it to anyone but himself, but dammit, he did *not* want to be here.

If not for the fact that reneging on his bargain with April would make him the biggest jerk in the world, Damien would have feigned a stomach virus. But then he couldn't claim a stomach virus six weeks in a row, could he?

He blew out a disgusted breath.

"Just suck it up and deal."

But telling himself to just deal with it was one thing. Being able to actually do that was something entirely different. Being back in this neighborhood reminded him too much of the person he used to be. It brought back painful memories, those he'd tried to let go of when he'd moved from the Ninth Ward with a vow to never return to this place that had caused his family such pain.

He'd bought that parcel of land, and had all intentions of building Alexander Quarters there, but that work would be farmed out to contractors. He could direct its construction from afar.

And, honestly, Damien didn't mind helping the kids at A Fresh Start find their way out of these streets, but that, too, he'd rather do from a distance. He didn't hesitate to support April's efforts financially, but he never wanted to be so hands-on.

Looked as if that was going to change, starting today.

Sucking in a deep breath, Damien started for the youth center. When he entered, it was as if the same soundtrack that had been playing when he'd come here earlier in the week was on repeat. The sound of young voices talking about the new Rihanna video and the latest celebrity meltdown on Twitter buzzed about his head.

He spotted April down the hallway. She walked toward him, but it was obvious she hadn't seen him just yet. Damien took the time to study her. There had been some sort of shift last night. He couldn't explain it, but he sure as hell felt it. The snug fit of the plum-colored T-shirt she wore affected him in a way it wouldn't have before the hours they'd spent talking while browsing through those art galleries.

It had occurred to him while he lay in bed, too wired to fall asleep, that the time he spent with April last night was the longest he'd spent just getting to know any woman without the promise of something more intimate happening at the end of the night. Not that he was a horndog with only one thing on his mind. He'd had his share of long-term monogamous relationships. But it was usually the case that once the evening wound down, there would be some action between the sheets. Apart from his coworkers, April was one of only a handful of female friends in his life who was truly just a friend.

But after the way she'd looked at him when he caught her midfall—after the slight shudder that he'd felt as he held her close to him, his arm tucked solidly underneath her soft yet firm breast—Damien wasn't sure he wanted her to be just a friend anymore.

He recognized the moment she spotted him. Her eyes widened, as if surprised.

"You're here!" she said as she walked up to him.

There was no *as if* about it. She *was* surprised.

"Of course I'm here. You thought I wouldn't show up?" Damien asked in a teasing voice, knowing damn well that it had only been minutes ago that he'd had to talk himself into not burning rubber as he hightailed it out of here.

April wiggled her hand. "I figured there was a fifty-fifty shot of you sticking around."

He slapped a hand to his chest. "That hurts."

"Whatever," she said with a laugh. She gestured with her head. "Come on. We have you set up down the hallway."

"Anyone signed up to take the class?" he asked.

She nodded. "You've got twelve kids, which is pretty good."

A dozen kids was more than Damien expected. Thinking back to when he was a their age, he probably would have laughed if someone had asked him to get up early on a Saturday morning to hear some guy he didn't even know talk to him about how to manage his money. However, when he walked into the classroom none of the students looked as if someone had dragged them by the ear and strapped them to the chair.

"This is Damien Alexander," April said by way of introduction to the teens, who sat at folding tables with notebooks opened in front of them.

"Mr. Alexander—" She turned to him. "Can they call you Damien? We're pretty informal around here."

Damien nodded.

"Mr. Damien grew up just a few blocks away," April continued. "He went on to college and then to graduate school, and today he's a successful businessman in New Orleans. Over the next six weeks he will share tips with all of you about how to save money—no matter how little you make—and how to start investing in your future."

Damien expected snide remarks, or even snorts of disbelief, but he got none of that. The kids seemed genuinely interested.

No, they didn't just *seem* interested, they *were* interested. It was evident only a few minutes into his discussion on the basics of starting a savings account. Questions were coming at him from every corner of the classroom, kids wanting to know what was the ideal minimum amount of funds they should keep in their bank accounts, which many of them already had at fifteen and sixteen years old. Some wanted to know about credit unions, which institutions made it easiest to access money in cases of emergency, how interest worked.

After about twenty minutes, Damien forgot all about not wanting to be here. Their enthusiasm was infectious.

Halfway through the session, the door opened quietly and April slipped in. She stood in the back of the class-room, a broad smile stretching across her face as she looked at the kids, who had become more excited and engaged with every minute that passed. After observing them for a few minutes, April gave him a thumbs-up before slipping out of the room.

Damien continued to check his watch, not because he was ready to go, but because the time seemed to be flying by at amazing speed. With five minutes left in the session, he brought the discussion about the dangers of payday-loan companies to a close and asked the kids if there was anything in particular they wanted to dis-cuss next week. He'd created a loose outline, but that was when he thought he'd have to suffer through an hour of trying to keep his students awake. That wasn't the case with this crew. They were into this.

By the time the last teen filed out of the room, Damien already had enough ideas flowing in his head for another ten sessions. He was buoyed by their enthu-siasm. He still didn't know the names of half of them, but already Damien felt a kinship with them. It hadn't been all that long ago that he had been one of them. He wanted to see them succeed, and if it meant sacrific-ing his Saturday mornings for the rest of the summer he was more than willing to do so.

"It looks as if that went well."

He turned to find April walking toward him, that huge smile from earlier once again lighting up her face, making her even more beautiful.

"Yeah. It went really well," Damien said, unable to rein in his own smile. "The kids were really into it. I thought it would be a struggle to get them to pay attention, but it wasn't at all."

"These kids are impressive," April said. "They caught on to classical music so quickly, you'd think they'd been playing forever. Do you want to grab a bite to eat at the café?"

"I was just about to ask you the same thing," Damien said. "A couple of the kids who just left the class were on their way to work in the café. They asked me to stop by before I leave. They're proud of their jobs there. And they're serious about it, too. I suggested staying around for another ten minutes to finish up a discussion we were having, but those who needed to get to work wouldn't hear of it. They didn't want to be late for their shifts."

She beamed. "They're awesome kids, aren't they?"

"Yes, they are. You all are helping to instill a solid work ethic in them." He caught her by the wrist. "Thank you for letting me be a part of it."

"You're one of the reasons we're able to do this, Damien. Your financial help is key to keeping this program going."

"I'm not talking just about the money. I'm talking about being here today." He hesitated for a moment before he spoke. "I needed this, April. I need to be here."

"What do you mean?"

Damien settled his backside on the edge of the desk and let his hands drop onto his thighs.

"You've probably noticed that I tend to stay away from the neighborhood."

"Of course I noticed," she said. "I figured it had to do with Kurt. And with your dad. No one can blame you for not wanting that reminder."

"It's not just about what happened to them, although, yeah, that has a lot to do with it. But it's about me, too," Damien said. "I didn't want to be reminded of what my life could have been like if I'd allowed myself to get caught up in these streets. Once my dad was killed, I became exactly the kind of kid he didn't want me to become."

"But you *changed*," April stressed. "You worked hard and you made a way for yourself, and now you're giving other kids hope for their futures, too. You're showing them that their zip code doesn't define who they are."

"Yeah, I guess I am," Damien said. "And that's thanks to you." He looked her directly in the eyes, knowing the conviction in his voice couldn't possibly convey the depths of his gratitude. "Thank you for forcing me to come here."

"I guess that means I don't have to worry about you trying to wiggle your way out of holding up your end of the bargain anymore, right?"

Damien nodded. "That's right," he said. "And speaking of our bargain, there's a fund-raiser at the Roosevelt Hotel next Saturday night that I'll need you to attend."

"The Roosevelt," she said, her brows arching. "I'm impressed."

"My wallet isn't," Damien said with a laugh. "The banquet is a thousand dollars a couple, but in the past the guest list has been a rundown of who's who in the city, so I'm hoping it's worth it."

April held up a hand. "Wait a minute. Let me get this straight. You're going to spend a thousand dollars to ask people to give you money? Did I hear this correctly?"

"You know the old saying that you have to spend

money to make money? Well, the same goes for finding investors. You've got to invest a little of your own before you find people willing to invest in you."

"Hmm," April murmured with a nod. "I like that. You know what I think, Mr. Damien?"

He laughed at the *mister*. "What's that?"

"I think I might be able to learn a thing or two from you."

"About finance?"

Her eyes dropped to his mouth and stayed there. "Among other things," she said, her voice low and warm.

The heat that began to move across Damien's skin had nothing to do with the temperature in the room, and everything to do with the way April's eyes continued to stare at his mouth. They hadn't discussed last night's near kiss, but based on the way she was looking at him now, Damien was tempted to bring it up.

He caught her chin and tipped her head up so that he could look her in the eyes. "There's a lot more I could teach you," he said.

A slow, sensual smile drew across April's lips.

"I'll bet there is," she said. "Maybe one day I'll let you."

April stared at the cell phone sitting on her coffee table as if the meaning of life would magically appear in a text message. Or as if it would bite her fingers off if she dared touch it.

She threw her hands up in the air. "This is ridiculous. Just call him."

She picked up the phone then promptly set it right back on the distressed ash oak table. She could not just call him. She needed to think this through, to consider the potential fallout to inviting Damien to her baby niece's christening party.

On the one hand, it made sense to invite him. Damien had spent his share of Sunday afternoons studying at the Knight kitchen table, so he was technically a friend of the family. Even though he was several years younger than her three brothers, Jason, Nicholas and Savion, Damien would often join them for a pickup game of basketball between study sessions. April doubted anyone would consider it strange that she would invite him to a family gathering.

But what if they did?

Her brothers all knew about her crush on Damien, thanks to Savion sticking his nose where it didn't belong and reading her journal just before she left for college. And because her brothers were the worst when it came to teasing their baby sister, they continued to joke about April's crush for years after.

"Oh, stop it," April said out loud to the empty room.

That was a long time ago. No one would think there was anything going on between her and Damien just because she brought him along for barbecue.

Before she could chicken out yet again, April picked up the phone and called him.

Damien answered on the first ring. "Hey, what's up?" His rich voice never failed to cause her skin to pebble.

"Hi," April said. Why did she have to sound so breathless? "I was, uh, just calling to see if you were free this afternoon."

There was a slight pause. "Did we have something planned?" he asked.

"No, no. I just… Well, Jason and my sister-in-law,

Shelby, are hosting a cookout today. Their baby girl is being christened this morning. I wondered if maybe you wanted to come along. If, you know, you're not busy."

The brief hesitation on the other end of the line seemed to go on for ages, even though it was only a few seconds.

"Give me just a minute," Damien finally said. "I'm skimming through what I have left to review on this contract. I should be able to get it done within the next hour or so. Should I meet you at your house?"

April was happy there wasn't anyone around to see the ridiculously huge smile that spread across her face. As a grown woman, she should not grin like a school-girl just because the man had agreed to join her for barbecue.

"Sounds great," she said. "I'll see you in an hour."

By her third wardrobe change April decided that she'd jumped right over ridiculous and was knee-deep in preposterous territory, but it didn't stop her from try-ing on yet another outfit. If she were going to Jason's alone she would have thrown on an old pair of jeans and a T-shirt and would have been done with it.

But she wasn't going alone. Damien would be with her.

"This is the one," she said, looking herself over in the mirror. She'd finally settled on a flowing skirt and silk tank top with lace trimming around the bust area. She tied her favorite scarf around her waist to act as a belt, and brushed her hair, leaving it flowing around her shoulders.

She decided that subtlety was the best option when it came to makeup. If she showed up at her sister-in-law's with a fully made-up face, Shelby would definitely take notice. She hounded April on a regular basis about her tendency to downplay her looks.

A car door slammed closed outside, and moments later came the rap of knuckles on her front door. April's heartbeat ramped up to twice its usual speed.

"Stop being so thirsty for his attention," April chastised herself in the mirror.

She gave her hair a final fluff and then rushed over to answer the door. She nearly swallowed her tongue at the sight that greeted her.

Even in plain army-green deck shorts and a yellow polo shirt, Damien was simply divine. His muscular biceps tested the limits of his sleeves, and April just knew the designer sunglasses tucked in the front of his shirt would look sexy as hell covering his eyes.

"Hi," she greeted, unable to stop the smile that stretched across her lips. She must look like an idiot, but God knew she couldn't help it. Just the knowledge that he was willing to join her at a gathering that didn't include a group of wealthy investors made her so ridiculously happy that April figured she'd smile for the rest of the day.

"Ready?" Damien asked.

She nodded and followed him out to his car. When they arrived at her brother's house in Metairie, there were already at least a dozen cars parked in their short driveway and along the curb surrounding the house. They parked two houses down, in front of a bi-level-style structure that was repeated every fourth home.

"When did Jason move to Metairie?" Damien asked as he helped her out of the car.

"After Katrina," April answered. "Their house in New Orleans East flooded. He realized the commute was about the same for both him and Shelby, so they moved out this way."

"Do they enjoy living in the suburbs?"

"According to Jason it's better, especially now that they have kids. Even though the houses are all pretty cookie-cutter, he likes having a bigger house and back-yard for less money."

"That's interesting," Damien said with a nod. "That's something I'll have to take into consideration when it comes to the project I'm working on, although I never really pictured families with young children living there."

"Really?" April asked. "I would have thought they would be your ideal resident. We need families with young children back in the Ninth Ward."

"Yeah, but—"

"Is that D-Dawg Alexander?"

She and Damien both turned at the sound of Savion's loud voice carrying from the front door. He jogged up the walkway and reached out to Damien, bringing him in for a one-armed hug.

"What's up with you, man?" Savion greeted. "It's been a minute since I've seen you around here. Well, except on the covers of magazines, Mr. Bachelor of the Year."

"Top Ten Bachelor," April corrected.

"Oh. Excuse me," her brother said. He squeezed her in a too-tight hug, kissing the crown of her head. "If I'd known you were coming I would have brought you a couple of bottles of my new beer," Savion said.

Damien's forehead creased in a frown. "I wanted to ask you about the beer since I noticed it in your fridge the other day. Since when did you start drinking beer?" he asked April.

"She drinks my beer," Savion said.

"My brother fancies himself a craft-beer maker," April explained. "I bought him a home-brewery kit for Christmas and now he has all these ideas about opening up his own fancy sports bar that only serves craft beer."

"That doesn't sound like a bad idea," Damien said. "Something like that would fit right in with the type of places I want occupying the retail space of the property I'm planning to build in the Ninth Ward."

April swung around to face him, her brows dipping in confusion. "It does? But I thought—"

"We can talk business later," Savion interrupted. "Right now, both of y'all need to grab a plate of the barbecue the Knight brothers are cooking up. It's off the chain."

They bypassed the house, heading straight for the gate that led to the backyard. There were at least two dozen people seated around the folding tables that Jason had set up in the backyard. April walked over to the one underneath the awning stretching out over the rear patio. Covered with a plastic pink tablecloth and trimmed with garland made up of paper crosses, it held a cake in the shape of the Holy Bible with a picture of her two-month-old niece, Naomi, airbrushed in sugar.

Her sister-in-law came up to her, followed closely by Jason, who held the swaddled baby in his arms.

"Hey there," April greeted. "How did the christening go?"

"She cried. As usual."

"Oh, hush," her sister-in-law said. "She's a baby. Of course she cried."

"I was talking about you," Jason said. Shelby swatted him on the arm. "Hey, hey, hey, careful now," her brother said. "I'm holding precious cargo here." He leaned over and placed a kiss on April's cheek. "Thanks for stopping by."

"Of course I came. I'm sorry I missed the service," April said.

"Don't worry, he recorded the entire thing on his phone." Shelby rolled her eyes as she took the baby from Jason's arms.

Jason held his phone up. "I'll upload it to YouTube and send everyone a link after the picnic." He looked past April, his eyes squinting. "Damien Alexander? Is that you?" Jason asked.

"Long time no see." Damien extended a hand and brought Jason in for the same kind of one-armed hug he'd shared with Savion.

"You're damn right it's been a long time. How have you been, man? How's Kurt doing?"

April cringed. She tried not to bring up Damien's older brother. She knew it was a difficult subject. But Kurt had been closer to her older brothers' ages, so it made sense that Jason would ask about him.

"He's doing better," Damien answered with less difficulty than April would have first assumed. "Stubborn, as usual."

"No one expected that to change," Jason said with a laugh. "Thanks for coming over, man. It's been too long." Her brother stopped short. He looked back and forth between April and Damien. "Wait a minute," Jason said. "Are the two of you here together?"

April's stomach dropped. She didn't like the cagey smile slowly forming at the edges of Jason's lips. April swore if her brother embarrassed her in front of Damien she was going to make Shelby a widow.

"Are you ready to eat some barbecue?" April asked Damien, pretending that she hadn't heard Jason's question as she turned to the table set up with several chafing dishes just to the right of the cake table.

Jason, the big idiot, just continued flapping his big mouth.

With laughter in his voice, Jason said, "You mean to tell me after all these years of April pining—"

Oh, God.

"Jason! Where are the forks?" Shelby called, stopping her brother from plunging April into what was sure to be one of the most embarrassing moments of her life. Although she feared he had already said enough for Damien to glean what he'd been about to reveal.

She was hesitant to even glance his way, but she couldn't resist the pull. She was sorry she did. By the look on Damien's face she could tell he'd figured out exactly what her bigmouthed, idiot brother was about to blab.

"Do you want some potato salad?" April asked, plopping a huge dollop onto his plate. "Shelby makes the best potato salad."

Please don't say anything, she silently pleaded.

Goodness, what had she been thinking, bringing him here?

She quickly filled her plate with food she no longer felt like eating, and made it out to one of the many folding tables her brother had set up in the backyard.

Damien followed behind, taking the seat next to her. When April chanced a glance his way, he was studying her with a curious look in his brown eyes. She forced herself to eat so that if he did bring up Jason's statement, she wouldn't be able to answer. But then, just like the true blessing her sister-in-law had always been, Shelby came over to their table just as she and Damien were finishing up their barbecue.

"Where's the baby?" April asked her as Shelby took a seat.

"I just put her down for a nap."

"Will she be able to sleep with all this noise?" Damien asked, gesturing to the crowded backyard.

"Honey, when it comes to that baby's rest, she doesn't allow anything to get in the way." Shelby turned to April. "Are you still playing at that place on Gravier tonight? A couple of Jason's friends were asking about it."

April nodded.

"You're playing tonight?" Damien asked.

Shelby answered for her. "She plays with this electro-soul group. You haven't heard them before? They're awesome."

"It's no big deal," April said, waving off her sister-in-law's bragging.

"Don't listen to her. It's a huge deal. She always draws a crowd when she plays," Shelby said. She jumped up from the chair. "Dammit! I forgot I have bottles boiling on the stove. Jason broke the bottle steamer yesterday."

"Do you need help?" April called after her.

She waved a hand in the air. "No. This is what I get for allowing Jason to touch things."

Chuckling, April shook her head as she stared at Shelby's retreating form.

"So, where are you playing tonight?" Damien asked, peeling the edge of the label on his bottle of beer.

"It's, uh, this little lounge on Gravier Street in the Central Business District. It's pretty neat. Styled after a London social club."

"What time?"

"The show starts at nine, but I won't go on until ten," she said.

He nodded.

"Why?" April asked.

He shrugged. "I just wanted to know exactly where I'm spending my Sunday night," he said.

"You don't have to come out to see me," she said. Her gigs with Electric Funk were meant to be relaxing. Having Damien there would be the complete opposite.

"No, I don't have to," he said. He looked up from his beer bottle, a wry smile tilting up the corners of his lips. "But I will."

The low-key entrance to the nondescript building between Magazine and Camp Streets belied what waited just on the other side. Damien felt as if he'd walked into an entirely different world. Or, more accurately, as though he'd walked into a building on the other side of the world. It was as if he'd crossed the threshold and stepped into a London club, leaving New Orleans behind.

Low-seated couches and chairs, done in an eclectic arrangement of various fabrics and colors that surprisingly didn't clash, but rather created a picture that blended well together, took up the bulk of the narrow space. Soft burning candles centered on the various sofa tables that dotted the room helped to set the laid-back, unostentatious vibe.

A crack of laughter brought his eyes to an alcove

just behind the entrance, where a foursome of twen-
tysomethings huddled close together on an ottoman
draped in the flag of the United Kingdom. The windows were covered by thick wine-colored velvet drapes,
their loose tiebacks allowing only a tiny sliver of New
Orleans to show beyond the double-paned glass. One
wall of the alcove was made up of Andy Warhol–esque
pictures of music icons like Jimi Hendrix, Mick Jag-
ger, Aretha Franklin and Van Morrison. The opposite
exposed brick wall held black-and-white shots of London streets, along with a large framed photograph of
the icon of them all, John Lennon.

In the center of the room, a spotlight shone on two
empty armchairs and two erect music stands. A deejay
stood behind a slim table just to the right of them, providing a smooth mix of early 90s R & B.

"You actually came?"

Damien whirled around and had to do a double take
at the sight of April standing before him.

What the heck?

If she'd walked past him on the street, Damien
doubted he would have recognized her, even though
she'd done nothing to change the appearance of her face.
It was everything else that was different. Her jeans were
well-worn, with several rips and tears peppering her
thighs, knees and shins. The vest she wore was equally
worn, the soft leather lighter in some places. She wore
nothing underneath it. No shirt—just bare skin.

Her cello was slung over her shoulder like a huge
backpack, encased in a dark purple nylon carrying case.
There was a bright yellow button that read Yo, Cell Out,
Dude! stuck to the front of it.

"I seriously thought you were kidding when you said you would be here tonight," April said.

"Why would you think that? I tried to see you play whenever I could in the past."

"Yeah, but that's when I was in my prime."

"Your prime? What, are you ready to collect Social Security or something?"

"You know what I mean," she said. "I'm not *the* April Knight here. These little jam sessions are just for fun."

"Well, that's perfect then. I always thought you played best when you just allowed yourself to have fun."

"Hey, April, we're ready." The guy who called to her looked to be about their age. He carried a set of bongos. A blonde woman with dreadlocks down past her rear end followed just behind him. She carried a tambourine in one hand and had a harmonica harness around her neck.

The trio went over to the vacant furniture in the center of the room.

The crowd, which had grown steadily since Damien had arrived, applauded as the musicians took their spots.

Damien found an available seat on one of the couches that faced the group of musicians.

April set the instrument case against the wall next to the deejay table and gave the deejay a kiss on the cheek before returning to the brushed velvet armchair. She positioned the cello between her legs, then leaned forward and spoke into the microphone that had been set up in front of her chair.

"Good evening, all you beautiful people." Her voice was low and husky, complementing the club's subdued vibe. "I want to thank you all for coming out tonight.

We're gonna just sit back, relax and let the music take us wherever it feels right."

She counted down and started with a sound Damien had never heard from a cello before. It had a jazzy vibe to it, with hip, swanky notes that had the patrons seated around the room tapping their feet.

He was completely mesmerized.

Who was this woman?

This was a totally different side to April, one Damien would have never guessed existed. He was used to seeing her in elegant evening gowns, playing to a crowd that was just as elegantly attired and who accepted the classical music that strummed from her fingers as if it was their due. This crowd bobbed their heads to the funky, eclectic beat, appreciation evident in the way they focused all their attention on the musicians.

They played for a half hour, with each member of the trio getting their chance to shine with a solo performance. But it wasn't about outshining the others. They grooved together, cheered each other on.

When they brought the jam session to a close, the crowd responded with as boisterous an applause as a group this mellow could muster. There were even a few whistles.

Damien just continued to stare at the woman he'd known since the tenth grade. At least he *thought* he knew her. But after seeing this side of her, it made him doubt everything he'd ever known about April Knight.

He stood as she made her way over to him.

"So?" she asked, her brow arched in amused inquiry.

Damien held his hands out. "I'm speechless."

"Uh-oh. Is that a good thing or a bad thing?"

"A very good thing," he said. "Honestly, April, I

don't know what I expected when I walked in here tonight, but it wasn't that. That was the coolest thing I've ever witnessed in my life."

The smile that broke out across her face was bright enough to light up this dim lounge.

"Thank you," she said. "I love playing here." She gestured with her head. "Let's go have a drink. Since you're a guest of mine, it's on the house."

They walked over to the bar at the rear of the room. Instead of the standard mirror, the wall behind the bottles was covered with sheets of brushed bronze metal.

April ordered two glasses of red wine.

"When did you start playing with this group?" Damien asked.

She tilted her head to the side. "About a year ago maybe? I've known Evelyn and Rolando for years. They're both classically trained, as well. They still play with orchestras, but when they're home, we try to get together for a show."

The bartender handed over their wineglasses, and once again, April motioned with her head for Damien to follow her. He walked a couple of paces behind as she led him toward a tufted chaise longue tucked away in a corner. He stared at her ass in unabashed admiration, completely drawn in by the way the soft denim cupped the delicately rounded cheeks.

Damien tried to summon a measure of guilt for staring at April this way, but guilt was the last thing he felt at the moment. He was intrigued.

And turned on.

There was something about discovering a mysterious new side to a woman he thought he knew so well that aroused his curiosity. And his libido.

And after witnessing that scene play out between April and Jason at the picnic earlier today, Damien's curiosity was definitely aroused.

Neither he nor April had mentioned it, but it had been on his mind ever since Jason spoke. He'd had an inkling about the way April had felt about him back in high school. He wasn't conceited, but Damien knew he'd inspired crushes in a few girls back in those days. He played football. He was popular. Of course girls crushed on him.

With April, however, it had felt different. Damien was sure her infatuation stemmed from something deeper. She'd admired the work he did in the classroom over the way he performed on the football field. The better he did in class, the higher her regard for him.

The thought that she *pined* for him, though? In the same way other girls had?

He'd hoped for it, but honestly, Damien never thought he was good enough for her. So he'd never bothered to pursue anything that even remotely resembled a romantic relationship with April.

Today had been a day of discoveries. He was eager to see what else lurked just beneath the surface.

When he sat next to her on the cushioned chaise, Damien deliberately sat closer than necessary, so that their thighs rubbed against each other. It was a test of sorts, to see if he'd read her vibe correctly, or if he was completely off base.

He wasn't.

Instead of moving away, April leaned against him as she sipped her wine.

"Is this why you're okay not playing with an orchestra?" Damien asked her. "You can get your fix here?"

She shrugged. "I never thought about it that way, but I guess you're right. I miss the live shows, but I don't miss the hassle. Traveling from city to city takes its toll on you."

"You look no worse for the wear," he said, allowing his eyes to travel the length of her. His mouth watered at the sight of the smooth expanse of thigh peeking through the rip in her jeans.

When his eyes met hers again he noticed the subtle heat staring back at him. Damien traced her bare arm with the backs of his fingers, the caress hovering somewhere between a friendly stroke and something…more.

"Do you ever think about going back out there? Joining another orchestra?"

April's eyes slid closed. Damien wanted to think it was so she could concentrate on his touch. She took a sip of wine before answering.

"Only on the rare occasion," she said. "There are some things I miss about the road, but I like being back home. I like being close to my family." She looked up at him. "And to you. I've missed you, Damien."

He swallowed. "Yet, in the two years since we've both been back home, I can count on one hand the number of times I saw you before I drove out to the center last week. Why is that, April?"

She shrugged her delicate, bare shoulder. "Life has this habit of getting in the way. If something is important, you have to make time for it. If not, something else will always come first." She caught hold of the hand that he'd been running up and down her arm. "We have to decide that our friendship is important enough to both of us."

Damien's chest tightened as he debated whether or

not to speak the words resting on the edge of his tongue. He decided to go for broke.

"Is it just friendship you're looking for?" he asked.

April's eyes flew to his.

"Based on what Jason said, I wondered if maybe—"

She shook her head. "Forget about what Jason said."

The hell he would. But just as he was about to demand they talk about it, she looked over at him with imploring eyes and said, "Please, Damien."

The multitude of questions that had been swirling around in his head all afternoon demanded that they talk about what her brother had started to reveal, but those two words, spoken with such earnest appeal, stopped him from pressing her on it.

"It's been a long day," April said. "I just want to enjoy my wine and the music and your company. But please." She put her finger to his lips. "No more talking tonight."

Damien stared into her soulful brown eyes, everything within him clamoring for him to ask her if there was any truth to Jason's words. But he tamped down the urge. There would be time to discuss it later. For now, he'd enjoy this rare evening with this woman who seemed to surprise him at every turn.

Chapter 6

The clinking of expensive bottles of champagne could be heard ringing throughout the famous Blue Room of the Roosevelt Hotel. Damien trailed his gaze around the opulent space, trying not to be overwhelmed or intimidated by the sea of wealthy partygoers. He wasn't some interloper. He'd paid handsomely for the opportunity to be there that night. He deserved to sip expensive bubbly and nibble on food he couldn't pronounce as much as the next person.

Yet, if someone offered to pinch him, Damien wouldn't turn them down. Who would have ever thought that the knucklehead who used to run the streets of the Ninth Ward would even be allowed to darken the doorstep of one of the Crescent City's most illustrious hotels, let alone rub elbows with such an elite crowd?

Damien had gladly handed over the one thousand

dollars it cost to attend this charity function for a local children's cancer foundation. It was obvious that the foundation's director, the daughter of a former governor, knew exactly the kind of people to target for tonight's event.

There were businessmen and -women representing every industry—from movers and shakers in the petrochemical sector to elites in the robust movie industry. Members of New Orleans's most prominent families bustled about, posing for pictures with each other, as if they had not seen the same faces at whatever society shindig they all attended last week. There were even a few professional basketball players from the city's NBA franchise towering above everyone else in the room.

While Damien enjoyed an exciting game of round ball every now and again, that wasn't the sport on his radar tonight. It was the owners of the city's local minor-league baseball team that he was most interested in rubbing shoulders with. Three of the four men who made up the McGowan Group were in attendance at tonight's banquet. He'd had a few minutes of Michael Berger's attention during last week's street fair, but his goal tonight was to get some serious face time with the men who could help turn his dream into a reality.

"This looks like the place to be for the rich and famous," April said as she returned to his side after a trip to the ladies' room.

Damien felt his breath quickening once again at the sight of her. He'd mentioned at the last minute that tonight's event was black-tie, but he knew April would be able to pull it off. The venues where she'd played in the past often required that she dress like this.

What he hadn't expected was for April to outshine

every woman in the ballroom. But she did. She looked stunning.

Her muted silver gown wasn't flashy like many of the others being paraded around the ballroom, yet its simplicity made it even more alluring. The silky fabric trailed over her curves with just enough give to not be considered slinky or inappropriate.

To be honest, Damien would have been okay with a little inappropriateness where her dress was concerned.

That thought would have shocked him just a few weeks ago, but it was par for the course when it came to his feelings about April lately. There would be no further denying it. Something had shifted between them. He wanted her in a way he'd never allowed himself to think about her before.

It started the night of the street fair, when he'd broken her fall on the crumbled sidewalk as he walked her home. He couldn't stop thinking about the way she'd looked into his eyes, or the faint shudder he'd felt as he'd held her close. It wasn't as if he'd never experienced such feelings before, but never with his longtime friend.

To feel this way about April was…different. But in a good way. A really good way.

The incident at her niece's christening celebration further solidified the fact that their relationship was on the brink of becoming more than just friendship. Jason's revelation, though prematurely cut short, had disclosed enough for Damien to put the puzzle pieces together.

He and April had yet to talk further about what Jason had divulged. Damien had heeded her plea at the club the other night, backing off the subject. But he wasn't willing to let things go unsaid for much longer. They would have to eventually discuss whether she'd really had feelings for him all this time.

And what that meant for their future.

"So," April said as she took a sip from her champagne flute. "Who exactly are you targeting again?"

"*Targeting* seems like a harsh word," Damien said.

"But accurate," she pointed out. "There's no need to sugarcoat anything, Damien. Everyone in this ballroom has a motive outside of helping to fight childhood cancer. The charity is what got them through the door, and thankfully, a group of much-deserving kids will be on the receiving end of some great benefits, but everyone knows that events like this are where deals are made. Which is why," she said, looking around the room, "I'm going to see if I can make a few deals of my own."

His head reared back. "What kind of deals are you looking to make?"

"You're not the only one who can benefit from connections with the super-rich. A Fresh Start is always in need of sponsors. I figure if these bigwigs can spend a thousand bucks to attend tonight's dinner, they can certainly shell out five hundred to sponsor new instruments for the music class and field trips for the kids." She looped her arm in the crook of his. "Now, shall we mingle?"

Damien barked out a laugh. "As you wish."

Once again, just as it had been at the Art for Autism street fair, Damien was blown away by the skill with which April worked a room. She had the perfect balance of self-deprecating charm and charisma that made people fall over their feet in order to heap praise onto her.

She must have honed those skills during her years of performing at ritzy parties around the country. She sure as hell didn't learn them growing up in the Ninth Ward. Damien was continually amazed at how different she was from the shy girl who'd sat next to him in English class. She'd grown into a bona fide social butterfly.

Tonight she was hitting all the right notes. And with all the right people.

John Hiraku, a tech giant who'd moved his microprocessor company to New Orleans several years ago, made up one-fourth of the McGowan Group. Damien had his team at Alexander Properties conduct extensive research on all four partners, and he knew it wouldn't be easy to lure Hiraku. The man was very deliberate in the type of investments he made. And, unlike the other three members, Damien couldn't find a single hobby or interest outside of business that he could use as a way to break the ice.

But the gods were smiling down on him tonight. Because, lo and behold, Hiraku turned out to be the biggest classical-music freak in the northern hemisphere. He'd reacted like a teenybopper at a One Direction concert when he realized he was in the presence of *the* April Knight.

"Ms. Knight, I'll have you know that I was in the audience the night you played Carnegie Hall," Hiraku said with a smile that stretched from Mississippi to Texas. "It was one of the most moving experiences of my life. You were absolutely phenomenal."

"Thank you so much," April said in a voice that oozed graciousness. She truly was a master at this. "That performance at Carnegie Hall was one of the highlights of my career. I'll never forget how it felt to stand on that stage."

"You were magnificent," Hiraku said, still holding

both of April's hands. He hadn't let them go since their initial handshake. Damien was pretty sure he'd hold her hands all night if April allowed it. "I hope you get the chance to play Carnegie again. I would fly to New York at the drop of a hat to see it."

"If I do, I'll make sure you're on the VIP list," April said with a wink. She turned to Damien. "Mr. Alexander here is also a fan of classical music. That's just one of the things the two of you have in common." She moved over a few inches so that Damien could get a little closer to his target.

"You both are also great visionaries," April continued. "Damien, maybe you can share some of your visions for the Ninth Ward with Mr. Hiraku."

Oh, yeah. She was really, *really* good.

"Yes, yes," Hiraku said. "You were telling me about your plans for the land just south of the Industrial Canal."

This was it. His big shot. If he could get Hiraku on board, the other partners of the McGowan Group should be a piece of cake.

"I have huge plans for the area," Damien started. "I would love the opportunity to deliver a formal presentation to you and your business partners, but I can give you a preview right now. Essentially, my plans are to buy out the homes surrounding the lot, tear them down and build an all-inclusive residential and retail building. My goal is to target young middle-class families and single millennials who are moving to New Orleans."

"*Excuse* me?" April said, her face a mask of confusion and disbelief. "You plan to do *what*?"

Damien released a nervous chuckle, but he ignored her question, focusing once again on John Hiraku.

"Structures such as the American Can Company in Mid-City and the Cottonmill in the Warehouse District have both successfully revitalized their neighborhoods. That's what I want to do with the Ninth Ward."

Damien chanced a glance at April. And what he saw staring back at him chilled his blood.

She no longer looked confused. She looked mad as hell.

April excused herself from the group of businessmen who had gathered around where Damien was holding court. She had to get away, because if she stood there listening to him describe his plans for their old neighborhood, she would deck him in the middle of this fancy ballroom. She'd just gotten a fresh manicure. She would not ruin it because of him.

April concentrated on slowing down her pace, lest she stomp out of the ballroom like an irate cartoon character. Although that was how she felt right now. It was a wonder there wasn't steam coming out of her ears.

As she made her way out to the Roosevelt's ornate hallway, April had to bargain with herself to calm down. If she made it through the night without ripping into Damien, she would treat herself to the white chocolate cheesecake she'd been craving at her favorite restaurant. She may even ask for extra whipped cream on top.

But white chocolate cheesecake couldn't possibly taste as good as it would feel to give Damien a piece of her mind. Her emotions ran the gamut from shock to hurt, but mostly she felt rage.

How *dare* he come in and do the very thing the people of the Ninth Ward had been fighting against.

Residents had spent the past few years fighting off outsiders who saw the period after Hurricane Katrina as a perfect opportunity to come in and sell off their neighborhood.

A clean slate.

That was how many had referred to it. The chance to push out the hardworking people who'd called the neighborhood home for generations, so that they could bring in a new, more dignified crop of residents. It had been a constant struggle between the little guys fighting to keep what was rightfully theirs and huge conglomerates that only saw dollars in their pockets.

April wasn't on the front lines. She had enough on her plate with A Fresh Start, but she fully supported those community members who worked diligently to save the Ninth Ward from the same gentrification other areas in the city had fallen victim to since Katrina.

Never once had she expected that they would have to fight off one of their own. She couldn't stomach the amount of disappointment swirling through her at the thought of Damien willfully throwing his own people under the bus.

"April!"

Speak of the devil.

She turned to find him striding down the hallway. April immediately turned in the opposite direction. She heard his soft pounding on the carpeted floors, but continued on, marching past the ornate mirrors lining the corridor.

"April, stop. Hold on," Damien called.

If she was one to use the F-word she would turn around and use it on him right now, fancy dress be damned. But she would not make a scene in this hotel. She would rise above it.

"Would you wait a minute?" Damien said, finally

catching up to her. He caught her by the wrist. "What's wrong with you?"

"I'm the one who should be asking that question," she shot back.

He looked at her with wide, shocked eyes, and April wanted to punch him in the gut.

"What are you talking about?" he asked, as if he didn't already know.

"Damien, I swear, I am so upset right now. It's best that you give me some space. You don't want to be near me."

"I'll give you space if you tell me just what the heck is going on with you. Why did you cut out of the ballroom like that? Everything was going perfectly and then you just bailed."

April whirled around to face him and placed her hands on her hips.

"If I'd known exactly what this big project you had in mind really was about, I never would have agreed to help you," she said. "In fact, I would have gathered up a group of people and started picketing outside your office."

The shock on his face tripled.

"You're not trying to help the neighborhood," April pressed on. "You're trying to destroy it. And you re-cruited me to help you!"

"Okay, calm down." He put both hands up and looked back over both shoulders at the people mingling in the hallway. "I'm not trying to destroy anything. Weren't you paying attention back there? I'm trying to build it up."

"No. You're trying to *change* it. You want to throw people out of their homes so that you can move in a bunch of new, more sophisticated people." She made air quotes around the word *sophisticated*. "It's called gentrification, Damien. And it's not going to happen to the Ninth Ward."

He released a frustrated sigh and rubbed the spot between his eyes. "That's not what this is, April."

"The hell it's not!" she said loud enough to turn heads. She lowered her voice. She had white chocolate cheesecake on the line, and she would not jeopardize it by losing her cool. Folding her arms across her chest, she studied Damien with a cool gaze. "This fancy building you're planning. How much do you expect a one-bedroom unit to cost?"

He remained silent. A muscle ticked in his jaw.

"Well?" April asked. "How much, Damien?"

"Our projections have a one-bedroom starting at fifteen hundred a month."

Her head fell back. She looked up at the gilded filigree decorating the ceiling as she husked out a tired, humorless laugh.

"Fifteen hundred dollars?" April asked, looking at him again. "That's more than some people make in a month. Who do you think will be able to afford to live there? Certainly not many current Ninth Ward residents."

"This is a good thing, April," he said. "It's going to bring in new businesses and a new crop of residents."

"It's going to bring in a bunch of high-end specialty shops that no one can afford. Why not help the farmer's market and community garden that just started up? Do you know what their mission is? To provide fresh, *affordable* healthy foods to people in the neighborhood."

"You don't have the entire picture," he said.

"No, *you're* the one who doesn't have the entire picture. You don't have *any* of the picture, because you haven't been around in years," she accused. "Honestly, Damien, when was the last time you spent more than an hour in the old neighborhood? Not counting the class at A Fresh Start," she tacked on.

He remained silent. That tick in his jaw became even more pronounced.

"It's been so long that you can't even remember, can you?" she asked. "Yet you claim that you're helping the neighborhood. You can't even bring yourself to spend more than a few hours there."

"You're one to talk."

April's head jerked back in shock. "Excuse me?"

"If you're this big crusader for the Ninth Ward, why did you buy a house in Bywater when you moved back to New Orleans?"

"What does that have to do with anything? I'm there every day helping to make the neighborhood a better place. Where I live is irrelevant. And how dare you try to make this about me," April said. She poked him in the chest. "This is about you, and how you're trying to destroy your own neighborhood."

"Stop calling it that. It is *not* my neighborhood," he hissed.

His words smacked her in the face.

Damien ran a hand across his brow and blew out an annoyed sigh. "That didn't come out the way I intended," he said.

"But it's what you meant, isn't it?"

He stared at her for several long moments before he said in a solemn voice, "I haven't lived there in well over a decade, April."

"Maybe that's the problem. You've been so far removed from it for so long that you don't feel any connection. You need to actually spend some time there, Damien."

"No, I don't."

"Yes, you do," she said. "I know it's been hard since Kurt's—"

He cut her off. "Don't go there."

April swallowed back the rebuttal that nearly escaped her lips. She knew his issues when it came to what happened to Kurt, knew that his brother's incident still weighed heavily on his mind. But she would not allow his demons to destroy her beloved Ninth Ward. Even if it wasn't her actual home anymore, it was still close to her heart. She would not allow Damien to bulldoze his way in there and change it.

She took him by the hands and walked farther down the hallway, to a seating area underneath the large arching skylight. She sat next to him on the tufted couch and took his hands into her lap.

"Why don't you let me show you around the Ninth Ward?" April asked.

She felt him stiffen. "I grew up there. I don't need a tour."

"Apparently, you do, because you don't realize just how much it has changed since those days when you grew up there. Or since Kurt was shot," she added.

His eyes flew to hers. That nerve in his jaw ticked at a manic pace, but he remained silent.

"There is so much good going on," April continued. "So much good being done. Maybe once you see how hard the people there are working to rebuild the neighborhood, you'll understand why the thought of you bringing in this new, expensive complex is such a horrible idea."

"That's your way of convincing me to join you on a tour? Calling my idea horrible?"

"Because it is horrible," she said. "It was one thing when I thought you were building housing for the people who actually live there now, but now that I know the truth behind this plan of yours, I can't help but think of it as being an extremely horrible idea. And I want to show you *why* I think it's horrible.

"Come on, Damien," she urged. "Be a tourist in your own city. Let me show you around the Ninth Ward."

He let out a deep breath and said, "Fine. I'll play tourist. But I'm warning you that nothing I see will make me want to change my plans. I'm going to show you how the project I have in mind will *help* the Ninth Ward, not hurt it."

April rolled her eyes. "Do you need me to break out the studies on gentrification?"

"I'm the one in real estate, remember? I've read enough think pieces to satisfy me for the rest of my life."

"And yet you didn't comprehend a single one of them? That's so unfortunate," she said.

Damien huffed out a laugh. "When did you get to be so sassy?"

Despite being pissed at him, she allowed a small grin to pull at the edges of her lips. "I've always been sassy," she said. "I just usually keep it under wraps."

Damien reached for her hand and trailed his fingers along her skin. Goose bumps marked the places where he touched her.

"Are you willing to return to the ballroom with me?"

he asked. "Your new best friend, John Hiraku, is probably searching all over for you."

"You sound jealous," April teased.

Damien's brows lifted. "Do I have reason to be?"

"Jealous?"

He nodded.

"Of Mr. Hiraku?"

He paused for a moment before he continued. "Not of Hiraku. But maybe the guy at A Fresh Start? What's his name? Simeon?"

The only thing that stopped April from swallowing her tongue was the fact that she would need it to eat her white chocolate cheesecake. That Damien would even care enough to be jealous of any man where she was concerned seemed preposterous. But the look on his face had gone from joking to serious.

"Simeon is just a colleague and friend," April imparted. "No reason to be jealous of him. Or of anyone else."

The sensual smile that drew across his lips held a hint of relief. "That's really, *really* good to know." He held his hand out to her. "Now, let's go back in there and try to get some investors for Alexander Properties *and* A Fresh Start."

Chapter 7

April stood just outside the gate that led to her walkway. She noticed Damien's sleek black car as it turned onto St. Ferdinand Street and motioned for him to grab the parking spot on the opposite side of the narrow roadway. He smoothly parallel parked, then took a minute to look around for something in his car. April continued to look on as he pulled a pair of sunglasses out of the compartment that dropped down from just above the rearview mirror.

She wanted to still be upset with him, but the minute he alighted from the car her anger from last night began to dissipate. He wore khaki deck shorts, a starched peach polo shirt and sandals.

God, why must he always look like someone she wanted to wrap up and tie to her bedpost? It made it that much harder for her to remember that she should still be pissed at him. But she'd always had a hard time see-ing the bad in Damien. Because she knew, deep down, that he was good.

She just needed to remind him of that.

As she watched him make his way across the street, she had to remind herself not to drool.

"Good morning," Damien greeted.

"Morning," April returned. "I totally thought you would stand me up today."

His brows lowered. "And here I thought you knew me so well," he said. He leaned over. "In case you didn't realize it, standing you up is never an option. You're just too hard to resist."

It took an unbelievable amount of effort to ignore the tingles that traveled along her skin, but April willed her-self to do it. She knew she'd read more into Damien's words than she should have. The same went for the way his voice dipped. If she allowed her mind to go where it *really* wanted to go where he was concerned, she would come out looking like a fool.

"Are you ready?" she asked him.

"What, we can't go inside for few minutes? Didn't your mother teach you to at least offer your guests a drink of water?"

"We're going to get all the food and drink we need on our tour," she said. "Come on."

She took him by the hand, paying no heed to how much this all felt like a date, instead of two friends just taking a casual stroll. But since he didn't seem to mind, neither did she.

They walked three blocks up to St. Claude Avenue.

"So, where does this tour start?" Damien asked.

"First, we're going to get that drink you talked about."

"I was only kidding about the drink, April."

"No, you were stalling, but that doesn't matter, because I've been thinking about this all morning. Not only will we have the best coffee you've tasted in a while, but you'll also get to see one of the most charming additions to the neighborhood."

They walked a couple of blocks east to Clouet Street and came upon a tiny building, no more than eight by ten feet. The sign bearing its name, The Coffee Shack, sat tilted to the side.

"Well, they got the shack part right," Damien said.

"I'll have you know that this little shop happens to be one of the best places to get coffee on this side of the city. We're lucky that the morning rush hour is over, because on any given workday the line is at least twenty people deep."

"For coffee?"

"Actually, it's for the owner's homemade cinnamon rolls, which are quickly becoming legendary."

April walked up to the counter of the orange-and-white shed and bought two tall coffees and one massive cinnamon roll. She gestured for Damien to take a seat at the single wrought-iron table and chair located just to the left of The Coffee Shack.

She set the cinnamon roll between them and handed Damien one of the forks she'd grabbed.

"Dig in," April said. "Breakfast is on me, since, you know, you paid a thousand bucks for last night's dinner."

His mouth tipped up in a smile. "Thanks for being so generous."

"Anytime," she quipped.

April waited, watching him as he broke off a chunk of the cinnamon roll. The moment he did his eyes slid closed and he released a moan that made her belly flutter with too many naughty sensations to name.

"Damn," Damien said. He looked over at her, his eyes glazed over with pleasure. "That's good. That's *so* good."

"I told you," April said in a singsongy voice. "We're actually lucky there were any still available. These usually sell out by 10:00 a.m."

"I want to buy a dozen and bring them back to my car."

She shook her head. "You can't. They limit four cinnamon rolls per person."

"What? That's crazy. Why would they limit what they sell?"

"It's not crazy, it's fair. Do you know how many people would buy them up? There would never be any left for others to enjoy."

"I guess that's the difference between us, huh? You actually think about other people besides yourself."

"You're not as selfish as you claim to be," she said. "There's a good heart in there. I remember it."

"Yeah, well, I don't know about that," Damien said. "That heart may have taken one too many punches to be any good to anybody."

April reached across the table. "Don't say that. You've always been so hard on yourself, but I know you. You are a good person, Damien Alexander. And not just because you have a fancy house and drive a fancy car and have a fancy office overlooking Canal Street. You were a good person when you lived in the shotgun house on

Desire Street, and stocked shelves at that little store that used to sit at the corner across from the church."

"You remember that, huh?"

"Yes, I do. I remember when a bunch of the kids from school tried to convince you to give them free stuff from the store. You refused."

He shrugged as if the way he'd stood up to their classmates all those years ago was no big deal, but April remembered what peer pressure felt like. Heck, she saw it every day at A Fresh Start. The technology may be different, but the problems and pressures the kids faced today were the same as what she and Damien faced back when they were in school.

"That took a lot of guts," April said. "A lot of kids would have caved under that pressure, but you did the right thing."

"You were a big reason for that, you know?"

"For what?"

"For me wanting to do the right thing, to be a better person. There came a point where the thought of disappointing you made me feel worse than just about anything else." He looked down at the half-eaten cinnamon roll, then back up at her. "But it looks as if I failed after all. I'd say you were pretty disappointed in me last night."

April's chest tightened.

"Try to see things from my side," she said.

"Wait a minute." He held up a finger. "Why don't you try to see them from mine, first," he said.

He pulled out his cell phone and brought up a computerized rendition of a seven-story building. The two bottom floors featured large glass windows that stretched from floor to ceiling. The remainder of the building was done in a dusty, reddish-brown brick.

"This is the building?" April asked, staring at the screen.

He nodded.

It was gorgeous, but it didn't belong in the Lower Ninth Ward. The building would stick out like a sore thumb. She looked up at him with a sad smile.

"You don't like it," Damien said. He blew out a frustrated breath. "Come on, April. How can you look at this and not see how great it would be for the community?"

"Damien, I just... I mean, look around," she said, stretching her arms out to encompass the area. "Can you really look at these houses and mom-and-pop shops and think that a building of that magnitude fits?"

"It's a vision for the future of what this neighborhood could be."

"And just what is that, Damien? These high-end shops that the people here can't afford to shop in? A slew of implants moving in from all over the country, jogging down the sidewalks and along the riverbank in their high-priced exercise gear and three-hundred-dollar earbuds in their ears? How can you look at this neighborhood and think *any* of those things would ever fit?"

She reached across the table again and caught him by his forearm.

"Instead of trying to change it, why don't you help make what's already here better? There is so much good happening these days, Damien. From Musician's Village to the Ninth Ward Community Garden—there are amazing rebuilding projects happening all over this area. And those projects could be even more amazing if more people invested in them."

"April, I hate to break this to you, but you're not going to get investors to put money into this neighborhood as it is right now."

"Not outsiders," she said. "That's why people from the neighborhood—people like you—need to step up and do it."

She sipped the last of her coffee and stood. "Come on. It's time for you to see more of what's going on."

They meandered past colorfully painted shotgun houses, all with well-kept lawns and several with residents either sitting on the front stoops or working in flower gardens. April waved as they walked by. She didn't know them by name, but their smiling faces were a part of what made this community home.

She and Damien arrived at the entrance to the Ninth Ward Community Gardens. The small garden was filled with people bustling along the rows of freshly tilled earth. April spotted one of the directors, Jodi Martin, standing next to a row of tomato vines.

She walked over to her.

"How's it going, Jodi?" April called.

"Well, look who finally made it back here." Jodi greeted her with a hug. The fiftysomething then used her teeth to pull off the dusty gardening gloves covering her hands. "Haven't seen you around here in a couple of Saturdays."

"That's because we've kicked off the summer program at A Fresh Start," April said.

"Oh, that's right. How is your little garden going over there?"

"It's still in its infancy stages, but the kids are diligent about its upkeep. Thanks again for the seedlings." April turned to Damien. "The little garden that's just outside the coffee shop at A Fresh Start? It was Jodi's idea."

April returned her attention to Jodi. "How have things been progressing here?"

"Just look around." Jodi stretched her arms out.

April could hear the pride in the other woman's voice. She was right to feel proud. What was once a wasteland of overgrown weeds and trash left over by the devastation of Hurricane Katrina was now a beacon of hope for the people of the Ninth Ward. Beanstalks, cabbages, tomatoes, peppers and a colorful array of other summer vegetables thrived in the rich onyx dirt.

This garden represented the neighborhood as a whole. Out of the devastation there stood hope. It just needed more people to help cultivate it.

Even though April had not been around lately, she did play a part in the upkeep of this project. She couldn't help but feel proud of how it prospered.

Jodi gave them a short tour through the gardens, including the area where they were hoping to install a new hydroponic reservoir. Once they ended their tour and exited the gardens, April turned to Damien.

"Now do you see what I mean? This is the type of meaningful progress happening all over this neighborhood. Doesn't it make you want to grab a shovel and get to work?"

Damien took her by the hand and entwined his fingers with hers, letting their arms swing lightly between them. April couldn't fight the excitement that flittered across her skin. Her blood warmed with an intoxicating charge of pleasure, its effect coursing through her. That the touch of his hand could make her so heady with desire was a testament to just how much she still wanted him, even after all these years.

But today wasn't about her long-held attraction to Damien. Today was about finding a way to make him see that his plans for this building were wrong.

She stopped walking and turned to face him.

"I want to know what you think about what you've seen so far," April said. "I want to know if you now understand why it's so important to support the efforts of the people in this community."

He looked down at her, an amused gleam lighting up his eyes.

"You always had so much passion," Damien said. He lifted his fingers and trailed them along her jaw. "Always wanting to save the world."

April's skin tingled where he stroked her. She fought the urge to lean into his touch.

"I can't save the world," she said. "But I can save this neighborhood. It deserves to be saved."

His expression hardened.

April took a couple of steps back. "You don't agree." It was a statement, not a question.

He remained quiet, but his body language spoke volumes.

"Tell me what this is really about, Damien. What's really behind you wanting to build this building?"

"I told you—"

"No." April shook her head. "I know what you told me, but I want the whole truth." She paused. Took a breath. "And unless you speak Kurt's name, then you're not telling me the whole truth."

The face that just moments ago held a smile now

held an expression devoid of any trace of humor. Once again, a nerve ticked in his jaw.

"What do you want me to say?" he asked. "That I still hold a grudge over my brother getting shot? That I blame these streets? This neighborhood?"

"Yes," April said. "I want you to admit it."

"Fine." He held his arms up. "I admit it. Kurt will never walk again because a person can't walk down the damn street in this neighborhood without a stray bullet hitting their spine."

"Kurt could have been hit by a stray bullet in a suburban shopping mall," she pointed out.

"But he wasn't. It happened here, in this neighborhood. The same way it happened with my dad. But I guess Kurt was lucky. At least he made it out alive."

April knew what she was getting into when she'd deliberately opened this can of worms, but knowing didn't make it any easier to deal with.

"I understand where you're coming from, Damien—"

He cut her off. "No, you don't. You may be from the Ninth Ward, but we both know our situations were different."

She couldn't deny the truth in his words. Even though they both grew up here, she'd had an easier time of it. For one thing, she was from the other side of the tracks—literally. The Ninth Ward was divided by a cluster of railroad tracks, and one side of it was vastly more desirable than the other.

"You always had more going for you," Damien continued. "You were smart. People knew without a doubt that you would make something of yourself and move on to bigger and better things."

"So did you."

"I had football. The only thing people thought about me was that I was screwed if I didn't make it to the pros."

"But you proved them wrong. I, on the other hand, was ridiculed and called a fool when I decided to go into music instead of medicine or law."

"You never would have made it as a doctor," he said.

"Thanks for the vote of confidence."

"Just telling it like it is," Damien said.

"My point," April continued, "is that we're both products of the Ninth Ward who made something of ourselves. And we're just two of the success stories. This neighborhood is full of them. It's unfair of you to continue to lay the blame for what happened to Kurt and your dad at this entire neighborhood's feet when it was the actions of a few bad apples." She squeezed his hand. "It could have happened anywhere. If you feel such anger toward this neighborhood, why come back to it at all? Why not just write it off completely?"

"Because you didn't," he said.

His words shocked her speechless.

"What?" April asked when she was finally able to find her voice.

"You came back," he said. "You didn't have to, but you did. Honestly, I'm sure it was a surprise to everyone that you did. You'd built this incredible life, traveling the world, playing at all of these historic venues. Yet, when it was time for you to settle down, you chose to come back to New Orleans and help out the old neighborhood. I realized if you could do it, then there must be some good that I could do, too."

"There is good that you can do," April said. "Look

around. Pay attention to what's already being done. This community needs people like you, Damien. Help build it up. Not tear it down."

Damien had a hard time focusing on the sights April pointed out as they walked hand in hand through the community now known as Musicians' Village. He remembered when news of the project was first announced. The neighborhood was the brainchild of two of the Crescent City's most famous musicians. They both wanted to do some good for the musicians who had been displaced after the storm.

But the beauty of the brightly colored duplexes wasn't enough to drag Damien's attention away from the thoughts that had been swirling through his mind for the past hour.

Was he making a mistake?

He truly believed that the complex he wanted to build would bring much-needed jobs to the area and help restore some beauty to what had become nothing but blighted homes and stumped growth. But what if it did price people out of the neighborhood? Was that what he really wanted?

When he'd first run across the listing, he'd sneered, thinking that anyone who bought that land would be wasting their money. But then the idea for the new residential building had popped into his head. There had been no malicious intent behind the thought. No scheme to undermine the residents of the Ninth Ward.

Yet, Damien couldn't deny that when he thought about Alexander Quarters, he didn't picture the people who'd greeted April and him with kind smiles as they toured the neighborhood today occupying the units. But even that hadn't affected him as much as the other thought that had begun to drum around in his head after April forced him to admit that he still blamed this neighborhood as a whole for what happened to Kurt.

He had no problem admitting to himself that he was still angry about his brother being shot in these streets. Sometimes, it felt as if he was angrier than Kurt. But he'd never tied what happened to Kurt to this new venture, at least not in the way his brain had begun to connect them since April had hurled her accusations.

Had he convinced himself that what he was doing was for the good of the community, when in reality it was some sort of twisted payback for Kurt's shooting? A way to push out the people who he unfairly blamed for contributing to his brother's incident?

Damien shook his head, as if the physical motion would somehow shake the thoughts out of there.

"I don't know about you, but that cinnamon roll we shared earlier has long since worn off," April said. "I could use some lunch."

Damien forced himself to table these thoughts until he had time to fully explore them. That is, *if* he wanted to fully explore them. He still wasn't so sure.

"What are you in the mood for?" he asked April.

She scrunched up her nose, then snapped her finger. "Oh, I know the perfect place. Do you remember that old building on the corner of St. Roch and St. Claude? The St. Roch Market?"

"Sure. It's been vacant for years, hasn't it?"

"Not anymore," she said. "It reopened a few months ago, and it is spectacular. Prepare to be blown away."

She started walking west, but then stopped at a bus stop.

"What are we doing here?" Damien asked.

"It's too far to walk," April answered. She looked over at him with a grin. "What, are you too good for the city bus?"

It was a trap. If he answered the way he honestly felt, he'd never hear the end of it. Yet, before he could come up with another alternative, like calling a cab, one of the city's RTA buses pulled up to the curb.

Damien had to admit that they'd undergone a huge improvement since the days back when these buses were his only mode of transportation. He actually enjoyed the short ride to the St. Roch neighborhood, which bordered the Upper Ninth Ward.

"Whoa," Damien said as they alighted from the bus in front of the large structure. "What happened here?"

"A massive restoration project," April said. "They returned it to its former glory, and now it's one of the highlights of this neighborhood."

They entered the white building with its huge windows and beautiful woodwork. The inside of the vast space hummed with the voices of patrons traveling from one vendor stall to the other.

Dozens of huge columns stretched to the ceiling, their bright white paint contrasting sharply with the dark wooden counters and stools that occupied the space between each set of columns. He and April both opted for Korean tacos, then took a seat at the tables set up toward the rear of the building.

"I have to admit, this is pretty nice," Damien said, his eyes continually roaming around the beautiful, airy marketplace.

"It's a lot better than the run-down place it used to be," April said. "We used to think the old building was haunted, remember?"

"Oh, yeah. It looked it."

April grinned. "Speaking of haunted, do you remember Halloween?"

"Mr. Johnson's haunted house," Damien said with a laugh. "How could I forget? That man was spooky as hell when it came to Halloween. I never got through the entire thing. I'd always bail halfway through."

"I never even tried," April said with a laugh. "The candy just wasn't worth it."

"You remember his house at Christmas, though? He used to go all out with the decorations then, too. It was beautiful."

"I think his wife was behind the Christmas decorations," April said. She sobered. "He stopped doing all of it after she died."

"What ever happened to him?"

She hunched her shoulders. "I think his daughter took him to live with her in Atlanta after Katrina."

Damien shook his head and huffed out a humorless laugh. "It's amazing how life can change in an instant, isn't it? I still remember that Friday before the storm hit."

"You were at Alcorn, weren't you?"

He nodded. "The semester hadn't even started yet, but football players had to report early. Kurt called to say that he and my mom were heading up to Hattiesburg. I called him a pu— A not so nice word," Damien said with a sheepish grin. "We'd never evacuated before. And the storm wasn't supposed to be all that bad, remember? But my mom said she had a funny feeling about this one, so the two of them left."

"It's a good thing they did."

"They would have both drowned in that house," Damien said.

April remembered the first time she toured the neighborhood following the storm. It had been months after they'd finally cleared it to allow residents back in. She'd stopped in front of Damien's old clapboard house and her knees had nearly given out on her. She could still recall the waterline, only a couple of inches from the eaves of the house.

"It's hard to see that so many of these houses remain the way they looked just after the storm," Damien commented.

"But that's what we're trying to change," April said. She reached across the table and captured his hand. "The Ninth Ward was all but written off by most of this city. But the people who live here refused to count themselves out, and they're no longer waiting for city leaders to take the lead. We're doing it ourselves, and when we're done, the Ninth Ward is going to be better than it ever was." She gave his hand a fervent squeeze. "Tell me that you can see what we're doing here, Damien."

"I see it now," he said.

And he did. Finally, he did.

Damien shook his head. "But I still believe in this project, April. I don't want it to die."

"It doesn't have to," she said. "Maybe there's a way to fit your vision in with what others in the neighborhood are doing. You can still build it, but change the concept. Make it affordable, make the retail shops something that the people in this neighborhood can use, and not something that will push them out."

Damien ran a hand down his face. "That's something to think about," he said. "It would provide jobs and housing, and it can still have the aesthetics I'm hoping for." He hunched his shoulders. "Who knows, this may work."

Damien realized that having her here right now was the perfect opportunity to finally bring up another thing that had been on his mind lately.

"Not to change the subject," he said, even though that's exactly what he intended. "But are we going to discuss what Jason said at the christening party, or am I supposed to just pretend I never heard it?"

"I choose option B."

"I don't," he replied, grinning at her quick comeback.

"Damn that Jason." April pulled her hands out of his grip and splayed them wide on top of the table, stretching them, then fisting them in a clear effort to get a grip on her frustration. "If he were not a new father, I swear I'd kill him."

Damien laughed. "Something tells me your sister-in-law would be upset if you made her a widow."

"She'd get over it," April said.

Damien drew a single finger across her soft skin. "Was there any truth to what he said?"

April sat back in her chair. She heaved an annoyed sigh, then looked at him with stark honesty. "What do you want me to say, Damien? That I had a crush on you? Is that what you want to hear?"

"I know you had a crush on me," he said. Her eyes widened with surprise. Damien shrugged. "Just because I was slow in English doesn't mean I was stupid. And, not to come across as cocky, but there were a few girls with crushes on me back then."

"Yes, that sounds cocky," April said.

He laughed, but then he grew more thoughtful. "I

figured it was just a passing thing when it came to you, but based on what Jason said at the christening, yours was more than just your run-of-the-mill high school crush."

April groaned. "I really don't want to talk about this."

"You made me talk about Kurt's incident. It's pay-back time."

She held her hands out. "Yes, fine. I had a huge crush on you. I helped you to pass English and you took pity on me and invited me to the prom. The end."

"Is that what you think, April? That I asked you to prom out of pity?"

"Well, didn't you?"

His mouth tipped up in a smile. "No." Damien shook his head. He folded his arms on the table and leaned forward. "I didn't ask you out of pity. I asked you to prom because there was no one else I wanted to go with more than you."

Once again, April's eyes grew wide with disbelief, but then they dimmed.

"There's no reason for you to lie about this after all these years," she said.

"Exactly," he replied. "So why would I?"

He leaned in even closer, caught her chin between his fingers and tugged ever so gently. His lips were only centimeters from hers when he spoke.

"If I'd known that your feelings for me were seri-ous, I would have handled things very differently back in high school."

Damien's heart began to beat triple time as his mouth descended on hers. His muscles tensed with arousal at the first brush of his lips against her sweetness. He pressed his closed mouth to her lips several times before his tongue began to trace along the seam.

Applying the barest hint of pressure, Damien pushed his way inside with amazing ease. The sweetest desire flooded his bloodstream at his first taste of April. He sought the crevices of her, his tongue roaming around, sampling. Learning.

Ignoring the fact that they were in public, he slowly and methodically explored her mouth. He'd waited much too long to do this, and he wasn't inclined to bring it to a close anytime soon.

But apparently April had other plans. She pressed a hand to his chest and pushed.

When she looked over at him, her eyes were wide with shock.

"What was that?" she asked.

"It's called a kiss," Damien answered.

She gave him a "No shit, Sherlock" look.

"Are you upset that I kissed you?"

"*Surprised* would be a better word," she said.

"Why are you surprised? You're a smart woman, April. I know you're not blind to what's been going on here over the past few days. You feel what's been happening between us."

"So, you've noticed it, too?" she asked in a shaky voice.

Damien leaned forward again, and pressed a kiss against her temple. "Yes, I have," he whispered into her ear. "I never allowed myself to imagine that something like this was possible with you, but lately it's all I can think about."

Her big brown eyes widened.

"What do you say, April? Maybe it's time we stop playacting, and see where this goes."

"Are you—" She stopped, swallowed deeply and then started again. "Are you sure?"

Damien couldn't stall the grin that tipped up the corner of his mouth.

"I've never been surer of anything else in my life."

Chapter 8

April was still several yards away from the open meadow in Armstrong Park when she heard the sounds of the flag football game in progress. She came upon the couple dozen men scampering around the grounds and had to take a minute to collect her senses.

They were shirtless. All of them.

She didn't think she had a thing for sweaty, shirtless men running around trying to grab a flag from each other's back pocket, but apparently she did.

She spotted Damien among the pack of players and instantly the others ceased to exist. There had never been a doubt that she had a thing for this particular man. She'd always had a thing for him.

And yesterday he'd kissed her.

April waited for the tingles she knew would travel across her skin at the thought of the kiss she and Damien had shared. Those tingles had popped up so often since last night. She craved them. Relished them. Because they signaled a change in their relationship. The change she'd spent more than half her life hoping and wishing would happen.

April took a seat underneath a tree, just to the right of the lighted archway at the park's entrance.

She put all thoughts of yesterday's kiss out of her head and just allowed herself to enjoy today. As she observed Damien playing, she remembered how much she used to enjoy watching him on the field back when they were in high school. Even though she'd never been much of a football fan, Damien made her appreciate the sport, simply because of what it had meant to him.

Football had been Damien's way out of his old life. April didn't want to think about what could have happened to him if he had not had the sport as an outlet. He'd been smart, but he hadn't started applying himself early enough in school to get an academic scholarship. Football had been his ticket to his college education and eventually to a graduate degree. Without this sport, Damien could have very well gotten caught up in these streets, becoming another statistic.

She shivered at the thought of that happening.

It was what she and her colleagues at A Fresh Start were trying to prevent with the boys who attended the program. She wanted them to all beat the odds the way Damien had.

April stopped short. She slapped a palm to her forehead, blown away by her own lack of vision.

"Why didn't you think of this before?" she said.

Football. That was what those boys needed. It could be the same outlet for them as it had been for Damien.

"Now to convince him to teach them," April murmured.

Once the flag football game ended, Damien and the rest of the guys on the field lined up to give each other handshakes. Once he reached the end of the line he jogged over to a patch of grass where all their shirts lay, picked up a pewter T-shirt and pulled it over his head.

Her body mourned a little over the loss of all that beautiful naked flesh.

He came up to her, a smile on his face.

"I thought I was meeting you at your place?" he said.

"I was thinking that we could discuss your classes over lunch," April said. "There's this great little Asian fusion place a few blocks from here. It'll be my treat."

"No way." He shook his head. "I let you get by with buying that cinnamon roll the other day, but you don't get to pay for my lunch. Ever. Consider it payback for all those times you used to do it back when we did homework together."

She rolled her eyes, but a part of her liked that he still remembered what she did for him back in those days. Once his dad was killed, things became even harder for his family, financially. It wasn't as if her family was well-off by any stretch of the imagination, but both her parents had well-paying jobs. It turned into a weird kind of game for her, figuring out the best way to pay for Damien's meals without him seeing it as charity.

He'd always been so damn proud, but he couldn't hide his circumstances from her.

Yet, look at him now. She was in complete awe of the man he'd become. He truly was the best kind of role model for her kids at A Fresh Start.

"I was thinking," she said. "We have about thirty

young boys who attend A Fresh Start, and while I've been able to convince some of them to take my music classes and Nicole has even gotten them into dance—although I think that's because they have a crush on her and want to see her in tights—there's still something missing when it comes to recreational activities."

Damien's eyes narrowed into slits. "What are you going for?"

She ignored his question and tried another angle. "Would you say that football helped to shape you into the man you are today?"

"Of course," Damien said. "Teaches discipline, responsibility, teamwork—" He cut himself off. "I know what you're getting at," he said. "Forget it, April."

"But just think of how beneficial this would be to those young boys," she said. "Not all of them will get to play on a high school or college team, but there are lessons they can learn through football that will help them throughout their lives."

"I can't believe you're pulling this on me," he said. He shook his head. "Give them an inch and they take a yard. My mom used to say that all the time. Now I understand what she meant."

April persisted. "It would be one extra hour a week."

"An extra yard," he countered.

"Would it help if I said please?"

His head went back with a laugh. "I'll think about it. For now, why don't we work on the project that you've already roped me into doing. I took a few minutes between meetings yesterday to capture notes in my phone. I have some ideas for the upcoming money management classes."

As they walked toward the entrance of the park, they

had to walk across the running path. They waited for two women who were jogging to pass, but one of the women abruptly stopped and turned.

"Damien?" the woman yelped. She jogged over to them and threw her arms around Damien's neck.

April would have been more mindful of slinging her sweat on someone if she'd been jogging, but she guessed it didn't make much difference since Damien was just as sweaty from his flag football game.

Great. She was being forced to witness two beautiful, sweaty people hugging in the middle of a park.

"Eva," Damien said. "It's been a long time. How have you been?"

"I've been okay, Mr. Top Ten Bachelor," she said with a pretty laugh.

April immediately hated that laugh.

Damien chuckled. "Please, don't bring that up."

They chatted for several moments about Damien's inclusion in the *Get to Know NOLA* list before he finally remembered April was standing with him.

"I'm sorry," Damien said. "Eva, this is world-renowned cellist April Knight. She and I went to high school together. April, meet Eva Gutierrez. We, uh…"

"We had a different kind of…ah…schooling," Eva said, her rich laugh saturating the air around them.

April wanted to shove a finger down her throat and make a gagging motion, but that would be juvenile. Maybe choking to death would have been a better option. At least she wouldn't have to stand around in the midst of the awkwardness that suddenly surrounded them.

"I should let you get back to your run," Damien said.

Eva nodded. "It was good seeing you again. You

should call me sometime. My number hasn't changed."
She winked and then returned the earbuds to her too
perfect ears and resumed jogging, her too perfect ass
looking way too perfect in her spandex running shorts.

Damien hooked a thumb in the jogger's direction.
"That was, uh—"

"Eva," she said, helping him out.

"Yeah. We, umm…we dated a while back. Well, not
really dated."

April put a hand up. "No explanation necessary."
Please. The one thing she did not want to hear about
was his relationship with the brunette goddess with
killer legs.

As uncomfortable as that was to witness, April was
actually happy that it happened. After their kiss yesterday she'd allowed herself to get so caught up in the
fantasy that had played in her head so often that she'd
stepped too far out of reality.

She was no Eva. And despite what Damien said last
night after their kiss, Eva was the kind of woman he
was used to having on his arm.

April couldn't allow herself to forget that. Damien
had always been out of her league. Just because she'd
shed the Coke-bottle glasses and baby fat of her youth,
it didn't mean she fit into his world.

What happened with the perfect Ms. Gutierrez a
few minutes ago was the perfect reminder to proceed
with caution where Damien was concerned. Yesterday's
kiss may have marked a new era in their relationship,
but she needed to take things slowly. The potential for
heartbreak was too great, and leaving herself exposed
would be foolish.

And if there was one thing that was certain, it was
that she was no fool.

* * *

"You definitely need an entire session on filing for financial aid, maybe two," April said. "We have a number of kids who never even considered college when they started with us, but now it's on their radar. Maybe we can set up a projector and you can take them step-by-step through the FAFSA application."

Damien stared at April as she sat across the table from him, several yellow legal tablets, colorful sticky notes and pencils laid out between them.

"Yeah, sure," he said.

He tapped a pencil on the tabletop, continuing to study her.

The change between the woman pre-Eva and post-Eva had been pretty dramatic. Where she'd been light-hearted, even playful before, she was now all about business. She had not stopped talking about his upcoming lessons for the kids at A Fresh Start since they sat down. She barely gave him a chance to speak, as if she knew Damien would bring it up.

And he would.

He couldn't sit here while a five-minute encounter with an ex-girlfriend threatened the progress he'd made with last night's kiss.

The waitress arrived with the array of appetizers April had ordered for them to share. As soon as she walked away, Damien said, "April, about Eva."

She looked up at him. "There's nothing to discuss about Eva. Unless she has some financial expertise, too. Do you want her to join you in teaching a class?"

Damien pinched his eyes closed and released an anguished sigh.

"Okay, let's just get this out in the open so that the

subject of Eva, or whatever other woman we happen to run into, can be off the table."

She cocked her head to the side. "Just how many are there?"

"Are we really going there?"

"You brought it up," she said. She held her hands out. "Let's have it."

"Fine," Damien said. He stretched his hands out on the tabletop. "We both know I haven't been a Boy Scout, literally or figuratively. I've had my share of girlfriends. And, sure, some of them probably don't qualify as actual girlfriends. More like just…uh…women I spent a little quality time with."

April put both hands up. "Okay, I changed my mind. I don't want to discuss this."

"Come on, April. All I'm trying to say is that I know how that must have looked to you, me and Eva running into each other. I can't change the past, but it doesn't mean I'm still that same guy who used to try to score with every girl I came in contact with."

"Here's what I don't get," she said. "You came in contact with me all the time, yet you never once tried anything with me. Why didn't I merit just a little of that kind of attention, Damien?"

"Because I never thought I had a chance with you," he said.

Her mouth fell open.

"Don't act so shocked," Damien said. "Why would I have ever thought there could be anything between us? First of all, your brothers would have kicked my ass if I'd ever tried to touch you."

"That's not true." She paused. "Okay, maybe that is true, but you could have taken them on in a fight."

Damien laughed. "Is that what you would have wanted? For me to duke it out with your brothers over you?"

She glided her finger through the swipe of red sauce garnishing the plate of fried dumplings. "Maybe," she said. "It would have at least told me that you actually saw me as something other than just a tutor or a classmate. Maybe I wouldn't have spent so much of my time being jealous of every girl you smiled at."

"I spent enough time envying the guys who were lucky enough to be on the receiving end of your smiles, too, you know?"

Her eyes went wide again. "Since when?"

Damien picked up his fork, then put it back down. He clamped his hands together, rubbing them back and forth. He pondered whether or not to say anything further, but it seemed only fair that he admit to his own bouts of jealousy where she was concerned.

"Remember that time you played the Hollywood Bowl and we met for drinks later?" Damien asked.

She tipped her head to the side. "What was that? Five years ago?"

He nodded. "I flew to LA for a meeting and found out you were playing for one night only with some orchestra there."

"It was a special tribute to Mendelssohn and Brahms," she said.

"I don't remember a thing about the music, but I remember that guy you were with. You introduced him as someone from the strings section?"

"Oh, was that—"

"Timothy," Damien said before she could answer.

Her brows shot up. "Wow, you remember his name?"

Another nod. "I remember his name. I also remember the way he kept his arm around you the entire time we sat at that bar after your performance. And I remember those looks he kept shooting my way, as if he wanted to punch me in the throat. I figured it was in response to the same look I gave him."

"You were jealous of Timothy?" she asked, as if it was the most absurd idea on the planet.

"You were dating him, weren't you?" Damien asked.

She gave a half shrug. "We went out for a couple of months, but it was never anything serious."

"I didn't care how serious it was. I just knew that this guy who shared your love of music and traveled with you on the road, spent several hours with his hand resting on your hip. And I wanted to kill him.

"I didn't even recognize it as jealousy at the time," Damien continued. "I just remembered feeling… I don't know…off, I guess. I felt off for days, and couldn't understand why. It wasn't until I put on one of your CDs—something I normally use to relax—and felt the rage starting back up again. It was as if I could hear Timothy's violin getting busy with your cello."

"Oh, my God," April laughed. She covered her mouth with both hands, but her eyes still glittered with amusement.

"You find this funny?" Damien asked.

"A little," she admitted. "I guess I feel vindicated. I never saw you as the jealous type."

"Neither did I," he said. "But, yeah, I was jealous at the thought of you and this guy dating. Even though I knew I didn't have any kind of claim on you, I still felt as if you were…well, that you were mine, in a way. You were my April. You always have been."

"Maybe you should have said something then," she said. "Maybe if you had, I wouldn't have had to kick Timothy to the curb when he tried to go a little faster than I was willing to let him."

Damien's hand balled into a fist. "What did he do? It wasn't that night, was it?"

"No," April said. "It was months later. And don't worry, those brothers of mine taught me how to take care of myself a long time ago. I kneed him in the kidney. According to the farewell email he sent me, he peed blood for a week."

"The bastard got off easy," Damien said. "I would have had him pissing blood for the rest of his life."

"Damien the caveman." Her lips curved in a sexy grin. "That's something I never imagined would appeal to me, but I must admit it's a little attractive."

He laughed, but then sobered. "All kidding aside, April, I don't want you to judge me too harshly for my past. Because that's just what it is, it's my past. I need you to see me for the man I've become. I'm hoping that when you look at me now, you see someone who's worthy of you. I want to see where this new thing between us can lead."

"You're sure that's what you want?"

He hunched his shoulders. "It feels right, doesn't it? I mean, *does* it feel right to you, because it does to me."

She nodded and smiled that smile that he'd come to love.

"It does," she said. "It feels very right to me."

Chapter 9

April sliced the air with the sharp baton as she flipped the virtual page of sheet music on her iPad. She concentrated on the violins. Their part in this concerto was, by far, the most difficult.

Her chest tightened with anticipation, and, okay, just a little bit of fear, as they got to a particularly tricky section.

"Easy, now," April murmured under her breath as they reached the vibrato.

The sound of the music flowing from their instruments was the most beautiful—if slightly off—sound she'd ever heard. April brought in the rest of the instruments as she directed the group into the concerto's soul-stirring conclusion.

"Yes," she said with a pump of her fist when they finally ended. "That was amazing, you guys. Wonderful job."

The beaming smiles on the faces of her young students brought April as much joy as hearing the music they'd played a few moments ago. She couldn't imagine what it would have been like for her if she'd had someone in her corner who actually appreciated classical music when she was their age. Everyone had thought she was wasting her time.

Everyone except for Damien, that is. He was the one who had encouraged her to continue her studies.

She could still remember that day sitting in the guidance counselor's office. Mrs. Levy had spent most of the morning trying to get her to fill out applications for several local universities whose premed programs had all been clamoring for her after April had scored a nearly perfect score on the ACT college admissions exam. She'd try to tell the woman several times that she'd already been accepted into the music program she'd had her heart set on attending, but the guidance counselor would not let it drop.

That is, until Damien barged into her office and asked Mrs. Levy if she had a hearing disability.

April had had no idea that he'd been right outside the door as he waited to go into the principal's office. He'd overheard the guidance counselor's badgering and had come to her rescue.

That day had been a turning point for her. Having Damien stick up for her and validate her choice to follow her love of music had given April the courage to stand up to her family. It was the day she'd made the choice to never allow anyone to discourage her from following her dreams, no matter how far-fetched they seemed.

She wanted to do the same for these kids. Especially Linsey.

April saw so much of herself in the young girl. It was as if the music called to her, the same way it had called to April when she was Linsey's age. She concentrated harder than any of the other students, and she played as if the music was a part of her.

No, not every kid had the kind of talent that it would require to do this on a professional level, but there were a few who had taken a true liking to it. Kids like Linsey. April wanted to nurture that interest as best she could.

"April!" She looked up to find LaDonna coming into the room with a huge smile on her face. "I have the best news," the director said. "I just received a call from the director of the Coming Home Project. They're in charge of the big grand opening for the groundbreaking ceremony on the new streetcar line that's going to start construction next month over on Rampart Street. They want your kids to play at the ceremony."

The excited roar that went up among the students was loud enough to lift the roof off the building.

"A well-deserved honor," LaDonna said. "Congratulations to all of you. You'd better get ready, because the spotlight is going to be on you."

Once LaDonna left the classroom, April clapped her hands and addressed the class.

"She's right," April said. "If we're going to accept this invitation—which we definitely will do—we're going to have to be prepared. This means extra practices. Are you all up for that kind of commitment?"

A dozen enthusiastic head nods had April laughing.

"Wonderful," she said. "Now, I know no one likes homework, especially during the summer, but this should be fun. I want you all to go on YouTube and find at least five different pieces that you would be interested in playing for the groundbreaking ceremony. Can you all handle that?"

A chorus of "yes" and "of course" and "we got this" rang throughout the classroom as the students started to pack up.

"Linsey, do you mind sticking around for just a bit?" April asked.

Once the class had cleared out, April took the girl by the hand and sat her down in one of the chairs that had just been vacated.

"How confident are you in your abilities?" April asked her.

The teen hunched her shoulders. "I don't know. I think I do okay."

Just as April suspected. She wasn't confident at all.

"Well, *I* think you have the potential to be an excellent cellist," April said. "And, because of that, I'd like you to perform a solo in the piece that we play for the groundbreaking."

"But we don't even know what we're going to perform yet."

"Don't worry," April said. "I'm going to make sure it's something with a solo." She looked the young girl in the eyes, hoping that if she saw the conviction in April's gaze it would instill some confidence in her. "You have potential. And you have a fire in you. It's the same kind of fire I used to see in myself. I don't want you to lose that."

Linsey shook her head. "I won't."

"Now, if you're going to perform a solo that means

you'll have to practice even more than the others will. You'll have to practice at home."

Linsey's eyes narrowed with confusion. "But I thought we couldn't take the instruments home?"

"No, you can't take these instruments," April said. "But I have an extra cello."

Her eyes grew saucer-wide. "You're going to let me have *your* cello?"

"Borrow," April said with a laugh. "Yes, I will let you borrow my cello. I'll bring it to your house this weekend."

"Thank you!" Linsey said with more enthusiasm than April had ever witnessed from her. She leaned forward as if she was going to hug her, but then pulled back.

"Thank you," Linsey said again. "Really, thanks a lot."

"You're welcome," April answered. Her throat grew tight as she watched the girl walk out of the classroom. She could only hope that she would come to believe in herself as much as April believed in her.

As she straightened up the classroom, her cell phone rang. Damien's name popped up on the screen.

"Hi," April answered. "I thought you had an all-day meeting?"

"I do," he said. "But I need a huge favor. I need you to come somewhere with me tonight."

April shook her head, even though he couldn't see her through the phone. "I can't tonight," she said.

"April, please, this is important."

"I can't. I have a job tonight," she said. "I'm playing for a gala at the New Orleans Museum of Art."

Damien's relieved chuckle came through the phone.

"That's perfect," he said. "The gala at NOMA is where I wanted to take you."

"Seriously?" She laughed. "How lucky can one guy get?"

"Hmm, I don't know. Maybe we'll get an answer to that one tonight."

April's skin flushed. Thank goodness they weren't using video chat.

"Tonight is a work night for me," she reminded him.

"The work portion won't last all night," he said. "What time do you have to get to the museum?"

"Seven," April answered, ignoring the flutters that continued to motion around her belly.

"I'll pick you up at your place at six thirty," he said. "See you in a few hours."

Damien stood near a piece of artwork he wouldn't have been able to identify if the artist were standing right next to him, telling him exactly what it was. It was one of several indescribable pieces in the New Orleans Museum of Art's famed Sculpture Garden. As far as he could tell, the metal structure resembled a dozen monkeys humping each other in the orgy to end all orgies.

But deciphering artwork wasn't his purpose here tonight. Like everyone else who'd braved the humidity of this sweltering summer evening, Damien was here to hear the harmonious sounds of one of the most intriguing classical musicians to make their way back to New Orleans.

As he stood several yards away from the dais that had been constructed in the middle of the gardens, Damien's attention vacillated from watching April glide the bow vigorously across the cello's taut strings to the mesmerized faces of the crowd who had gathered to hear her.

He was simply in awe of how far she'd come. He could still remember attending her very first concert, a poorly attended function at a small local theater in Baton Rouge. The only classical music he'd heard up until that point was in snippets used in movies and television commercials, but it was during April's first concert that he'd first started to appreciate it.

Her music had come to mean so much to him since that time. It was how he centered himself when life started to feel unbalanced. For years, when he felt himself getting stressed out, he'd slip in one of April's CDs, pour himself a whiskey and just let the music soothe him.

Just as she had the very first time he'd watched her play, and every single time since, April held him spellbound. Her delicate fingers plucked gently at the strings, releasing a melody in the air that captured the essence of the night.

"Amazing, isn't she?"

Damien turned to find Michael Berger standing next to him.

"Yes, she is," Damien answered with a smile. "She's one of the best."

"John Hiraku came into the office on Monday as excited as a kid in a candy store after meeting her at the Roosevelt this past weekend. He had no idea she was a native New Orleanian. She truly is a treasure to this city."

"I agree," Damien said.

His attention still squarely on April, Michael Berger folded his arms across his chest. "I've been researching the area you mentioned when we spoke at that autism fund-raiser a few weeks ago," he said. "There's a good bit of land available there. I've had my people looking into the work that's been done on the levees surrounding the Industrial Canal."

"The Army Corps of Engineers has done excellent work rebuilding them," Damien said. "The levees are all at or above national standards."

"Yes, that's what I've been told. It makes the area more attractive than I first thought it would be." He looked over at Damien, his brow raised, the barest hint of a smile stretching across his thin lips. "We'll be in touch, Mr. Alexander."

With that, Berger strode over to the statue of a nude woman clutching a blanket.

Damien wasn't sure how he should feel about the businessman's parting remarks. He'd been in this weird place ever since the day he and April toured the Ninth Ward. On the one hand, he was more excited than ever about plowing ahead with his plans to build the residential complex, but he no longer felt the same way about how exactly the space should be used. Witnessing with his own eyes the various projects taking place around the neighborhood had affected him in a way Damien never thought possible.

April's piece finished with a hauntingly beautiful last note. It was followed by a thunderous applause that surprised him. Not that she didn't deserve the rousing ovation, but Damien would never have expected it from the type of people attending the gala. Obviously they recognized that they were in the presence of greatness and couldn't control their enthusiasm.

He watched her accept vigorous handshakes from

several guests. She looked absolutely stunning in her gown of gold satin overlaid with black lace. The delicate trim of the sleeveless gown edged along her bust, cradling her perfectly sized breasts.

Damien forced himself to redirect his thoughts. If his brain remained on this trajectory he would need to find a quiet place away from the guest where he could get the situation burgeoning in his pants under control. As the crowd surrounding April finally thinned, Damien made his way to her.

"You're the belle of the ball tonight," he said.

Her light laugh carried in the same way her music had. "I don't know about that," she said.

"I do. You've charmed the pants off just about everyone here. They all want to be close to the amazing April Knight."

"Including you?" she asked.

"Definitely me," Damien answered.

She moved from the cello stand and took him by the hand. "I can use a breather," she said. "If I have to smile again in the next ten minutes, I'm afraid my face will crack."

Chuckling, Damien tucked her arm in the crook of his and started down the path surrounding the museum grounds. The night was still humid, but the closer they got to the water, the cooler the air became. They walked along the bridge that edged the south end of the museum.

"This is good for now," April said. She rested her arms on the balustrade and stared across the lagoon.

"I always wanted to go on one of those," she said. She nudged her chin toward the gondola gliding its way across the calm waters. "I've played in Venice twice, but I was only there for a day each time. I never got the chance to take a gondola ride around the city."

"That's the one thing about your job that I always envied," Damien said. "How you were able to see the world. Even now that I have the means to do it, I don't have the time."

"Make the time," she said.

His brow arched. "You think it's that easy?"

April shook her head. "I know it isn't. I've been lucky. My music has taken me to five continents and dozens of cities around the world, but it's different when you're going for work," she said. "You see it, but you don't really see it, you know?"

He came to stand behind her, placing a hand on either side of where her hands still gripped the stone railing.

"I wouldn't mind taking the time off to finally start exploring the world if I knew I wouldn't have to do it alone," Damien said.

She looked at him over her shoulder. "Are you inviting me to tour the world with you?"

"What if I am? How would you answer?"

She turned within the cocoon his arms created and faced him. "I would say that it's proof that teenage dreams really do come true."

Damien shook his head, expelled a sigh of disbelief. "Why didn't you say anything all those years ago, April? If you'd just told me how you felt, we could have come to this place in our relationship a long time ago."

She shook her head. "No, we couldn't have, because I wasn't ready." She placed a hand on his chest. "I wasn't ready to admit how I felt about you all those years ago. I needed all the life experiences I've had in order to be comfortable enough to say this."

"Say what?" Damien asked.

"That I want you," she said. She placed a kiss against his neck, just under his chin. "I need you…in *that* way."

Damien's groin began to throb with need. He pulled in a deep breath and let it out slowly.

"Have you taken care of all the business you needed to take care of tonight?" April asked in a low voice.

He swallowed and nodded. He wasn't capable of speaking at the moment.

"So have I," she said. She looked at him, her eyes liquid pools of desire and lust. "Do you mind if we leave?"

Damien shook his head. "Hell, no. As long as wherever we end up, we end up there together."

"Your place," she said. "Let's go."

As sweet as the music she'd played earlier had been to his ears, those two words were even sweeter. Damien grabbed her by the wrist and headed straight for his car. Right now, nothing mattered more than getting them to his house as quickly as he could.

Although they probably lived the same distance from the museum, April had suggested they go to Damien's house because in the two years since he'd been back, she had yet to set foot in his home. That bothered her, especially when she thought about the women who had probably been here. Women like Perfect Eva.

No.

She was not bringing thoughts of Eva or any of Damien's past girlfriends here tonight. This was *her* time.

When April entered his ridiculously gorgeous Queen Anne home just a block from St. Charles Avenue, she had to fight to keep her jaw from dropping to the hardwood floors. The ceilings soared at least twelve feet high, with two Corinthian columns creating the appearance of an entryway into the living room. A gorgeous white stone fireplace took up one wall of the expansive room, while the other side opened into a huge kitchen.

April did a slow turn, taking it all in.

Damien came up behind her and clasped her upper arms. He nuzzled his nose in her hair, just behind her ear.

"I hate to kill the mood," April started.

"Then don't." He nuzzled a little more, then asked, "What's wrong?"

"It bothers me that you never invited me here."

Damien ran his hands down her bare arms. "I have no excuse," he said. "I should have done so a long time ago. I promise to give you the complete tour. Later," he tacked on.

She turned to face him. "Honestly, I have no right to be upset. You visited my house for the first time just a few weeks ago."

Damien leaned forward until their foreheads met. "We should both admit that we've sucked at this friendship thing for the past couple of years."

April nodded. "But now we get to make up for it."

The sexy smile that drew across his lips sent shivers down her spine. Damien reached down and gathered her into his arms, lifting her and carrying her over to the empty dining room table.

"Really?" April said when he set her on the polished wood. "The dining room table?"

"It's a fantasy of mine," he said. "Indulge me."

She wrapped her arms around his neck and pulled him in for a deep kiss. Her tongue plunged inside his mouth with a vigor she'd never displayed during lovemaking in the past. Probably because she'd never wanted someone as badly as she wanted him.

April locked her hand at the back of his head and held him to her. Heat suffused her bloodstream as she fastened her mouth to his, savoring his erotic flavor.

She felt Damien's fingers tremble as he lowered the zipper down her back. The gown fell from her bust, leaving her upper body bare, save for the sheer and lace demi-bra.

A groan tore from Damien's throat as his hands clamped on to her breast. He cupped the mounds in each hand, tweaking her nipples through the sheer fabric. When he dipped his head and licked at the hardening buds, April let her head fall back and thrust her chest into his mouth.

"God, you're beautiful," he breathed in an awed voice.

One hand traveled down the front of her torso, inching past where the dress bunched at her waist, while his other continued its sweet torture, pinching and plucking her nipples, triggering a flood of arousal that coursed through her. His fingers found their way to the entrance of her damp core, but he didn't enter. Instead, he cupped her and pressed with gentle but firm pressure.

April rocked against his hand, her legs widening to give him better access. She undulated with increasing speed, lifting up slightly so that the base of his hand hit her cleft.

"Oh," she breathed deeply, tucking her chin against his neck and jerking her hips back and forth. She humped his hand at a fevered pace. The makings of an orgasm sat low in her belly, building with each second that passed.

"Come for me," Damien said. He coated two fingers with her moisture and slipped them inside of her.

April let out a gasp. She rode his fingers hard, her hips bucking wildly. He pumped his fingers in and out like a piston, grabbed the back of her head with his other hand and crashed their mouths together. The mere taste of him set her afire. The walls of her sex contracted around his fingers as she shuddered in his arms.

April slumped forward, her body limp from the shattering orgasm.

"How about we move this to my bedroom?" Damien whispered against her temple.

"You'll have to give my legs a moment to recover," April said with a ragged laugh.

"Nah. That won't be necessary."

He scooped one arm underneath her knees and cradled her back with the other. He carried her down a wide hallway, stopping before the very last door and opening it with a gentle kick.

April took a moment to register the four-poster bed in the center of the room just before Damien turned and lowered her onto it. He leaned over her and pressed a kiss between her breasts.

"I love this gown you're wearing, but it has to go."

He hooked his thumbs in the fabric that had bunched around her hips and pulled the gown down her legs, leaving her in her demi-bra, matching panties, garters and stockings.

Damien stood at the edge of the bed, staring down at her, his mouth agape.

"What's wrong?" April asked.

"Not a damn thing." He shook his head. He pointed to a seating area just to the right of the bureau. "Part of me wants to sit over there and just stare at you while I jerk off, but another part of me really wants to come inside of you."

April's sex clenched.

"Get naked and get in this bed," she ordered.

Damien's mouth curled up in a sexy grin. "Yes, ma'am."

He made quick work of his button-down shirt and slacks, shucking them on the chairs that she would definitely not allow him to sit on for the rest of the night. She wanted him in the bed.

He stalked over to the bed, his erection jutting out in front of him. She tracked him as he went over to the nightstand and pulled out a sleeve of condoms. He ripped one of the foil packets open and rolled on the latex.

He was taking much too long to get ready, yet she loved the anticipation. It drove her wild with want. The panties she still wore were soaking wet with her moisture. She squeezed her legs together to relieve the pressure building between her thighs.

"Damien, please," April pleaded.

"Don't worry," he said. "I can't wait another minute."

He climbed onto the bed and unhooked her demi-bra, tugging it away from her skin and flinging it off the bed. Then he hooked his thumbs at the sides of her panties and pulled them down her legs.

"The rest of it stays on," he said.

April looked down, unbelievably turned on at the sight of her body clad only in the garter and stockings.

Damien lifted her legs and rested her calves on his shoulders.

"I hope you didn't have any plans for tomorrow, because I plan to wear you out tonight."

With that he slid inside her, plunging his thickness to the hilt. April released a desperate moan at the sheer pleasure that stalked through her bloodstream. She arched her back, thrusting against him as he continued to pound into her, his strokes long and sure, and so gloriously deep he touched her soul.

She felt another orgasm building deep within her belly. Her limbs shook with it, the muscles growing heavy. She threw her head back as Damien thrust his hips with increasing power.

How long had she dreamed of this? How many nights had she fallen asleep and imagined this very thing happening? Damien above her, his hard length buried inside of her, deliciously stretching her body.

She relished every second. She wanted it to be like this between them. Always.

Damien changed his angle, dropping one of her legs from his shoulder and stretching the other one higher. Every inch of his hardness penetrated her. He drove himself deep, over and over and over again, until April finally flew apart, her body shaking with the force of the orgasm that ripped through her.

After several more thrusts, Damien's body stiffened and he found his release, his arms shaking as he dropped her leg and collapsed on the bed next to her. His chest heaved with the force of the deep breaths he had to take.

He rose from the bed and went into the bathroom, returning without the condom. Then he climbed in the bed and scooped her up against him, spooning her back-side against his front.

April let out a pleasurable moan. She was still too worn-out to speak in actual words.

"I have one question for you," he whispered against her ear.

"Hmm?" she murmured.

"Were you really done with your performance to-night, or did you want me so badly that you skipped out on them?"

She chuckled, turning around in his arms. "I'll admit that I wanted you badly, but not enough to put a mark on my professional reputation. I take that kind of thing seriously, you know."

"Yeah, I know," he said. He trailed his fingers down her hair and along her jawline. "Although, from what I witnessed tonight, you could stand up in the middle of a performance and curse out everyone in the audience and they would still love you."

April let out a laugh.

"I'm serious," Damien said. "They worship you."

"I've been pretty lucky. It's been that way my en-tire career."

"Do you know how amazing you are?" Damien said. He held the back of her head and stared into her eyes. "Look at all you've accomplished. And now you're add-ing to that legacy with the work you're doing at A Fresh Start. Is there anything you can't do?"

"Not so fast," April said. "My legacy isn't complete just yet."

"What else is there to do?"

"Boston," she answered simply. Damien's forehead creased with confusion.

"You've never been to Boston?"

"Oh, I've been many times. But I've never played with them. The Boston Pops has been my dream since the concert I watched on PBS when I was ten years old. That concert is the entire reason I wanted to play the cello. Just the chance to audition with them would be amazing."

"That's a great little story," Damien said. "But whether or not you ever get to play with the Boston Pops is not going to determine your legacy. It's already established. You're awesome. Deal with it."

Laughing, she wrapped her arms around his neck and rolled on top of him. Straddling his sides, she dipped her head for a kiss, and at the same time wrapped her hands around his thickening erection.

She whispered against his lips, "I'd rather deal with this."

Chapter 10

"Damien? Damien, where are you?"

Hearing April's voice grow closer with her approach, Damien pressed Send on the text message he'd just answered and quickly stuffed the phone in his pocket.

"Hey," April said, walking into his home office. "I thought you were trying to hide from me."

"Why would I do that?" Damien asked, strolling up to her and wrapping his arms around her waist.

She was dressed in the button-down shirt he'd worn last night, seeing as all she had was her ball gown. Damien would have been perfectly okay with her wearing nothing but the garter and stockings, but she'd nixed that idea.

They'd spent a lazy Sunday relaxing at his home, making love twice more, then feeding each other pad thai he'd had delivered from one of his favorite neighborhood restaurants. Damien could have spent the rest of the day and night doing a repeat, but the plans he'd made a few minutes ago would put him in the romance hall of fame.

He caressed the small of her back with his thumbs and nuzzled the spot behind her ear. It was quickly becoming his favorite place on her body. Well, one of them, at least.

"Why don't we drive over to your place so you can get dressed, then I have a surprise."

She pulled away from him, her brow arched with interest.

"What kind of surprise?"

"Why do people always ask that? If I told you, it wouldn't be a surprise." He slapped her backside. "Just trust me on this."

April had no other choice than to put on her ball gown from last night. It was out of place, even for a Sunday. They quickly drove over to her home in the Bywater, and thankfully found a parking spot just steps from the walkway leading up to her house.

She changed into a lilac sundress with spaghetti straps and a neckline that dipped slightly in the center, giving just a small glimpse of the tantalizing shadow between her breasts. Damien had to fight to stick with the plans he'd made. Right now, all he wanted to do was carry her to her bed and give a repeat performance of last night.

"Ready?" April asked.

Damien held in a sigh. "Yeah, I'm ready," he said.

They headed up Esplanade Avenue. It wasn't until they'd crossed Broad Street that April turned to him and asked, "Are you going back to the museum?"

Damien remained silent, but a smile edged up the side of his mouth.

"Damien?"

"Patience," he answered.

Damien could tell when she finally caught on, just as he turned onto Friedrichs Avenue.

"You didn't!" April gasped.

He turned to the parking area near the dock of the City Park gondola. "Last night you said you always wanted to take one," he told her.

"How did you do this?" April asked. "I've read that the guy who operates the gondola is booked up months in advance."

"I'm not revealing my secrets," Damien said.

Besides, he'd rather keep her guessing than admit that it was luck, a last-minute cancellation and an extra hundred bucks that made this happen.

After parking, he rounded the car and opened her door for her. Holding out a hand, he said, "Your boat ride awaits."

Less than five minutes into their ride, Damien decided that the gondola operator had not only earned the extra hundred bucks, but would get a hefty tip once the hour-long ride was over. He'd made it so that Damien and April rode in style. They gently sliced through the calm waters of the lagoon, with soft music playing through speakers hidden somewhere behind them in the long boat, and a bottle of champagne on ice for their enjoyment.

April snuggled up next to him, her head resting on his shoulder.

"This is perfect," she said to him. "Better than Venice."

"I wouldn't say that." Damien laughed. "Not that I've been before, but from everything I've seen in movies and pictures, Venice is one of the most romantic cities in the world."

"So is New Orleans," she countered. She scooted even closer, her back leaning against his chest. "Besides, it's not the city that makes it romantic, it's the company." She looked up at him. "It's still unbelievable to think that I'm here with you like this."

"It's not so hard for me to believe," he said. "In fact, I don't know of anything that could be more right than being here with you like this." He nuzzled her neck. "I look forward to evenings like this for a long, long time to come."

But as he thought about spending evenings like this with April for years to come, Damien couldn't help but think about how it would affect them if he went through with Alexander Quarters. Would April finally come around, or would it drive a wedge between them?

Maybe there wouldn't be anything to come between them.

Over the past few days, the more Damien thought about his project, the less his original vision appealed to him. He'd be the first to admit that he was stubborn, but these past few weeks had gotten through even his stubborn head. There was merit to everything April had said to him. He could do more for the Ninth Ward by helping the people here with a place that would provide safe, affordable housing than something that would price them out.

Damien still wasn't sure if this was exactly what he wanted to do. He'd already put so much into his plans, but with every passing day all he could think about was how much he would be hurting the people of the Ninth Ward instead of helping them.

And how much he didn't want to disappoint the woman resting in his arms.

Damien stood just outside the dark cherrywood doors with matching gold-plated handles. He'd gotten the call from Michael Berger just after nine this morning, asking if he could meet with the McGowan Group at their offices to discuss Alexander Quarters.

The project had been on his mind all night. After his gondola ride with April, followed by the most pleasurable thank-you he'd ever received in his life, Damien had arrived back at his house only to find that he was too wired to sleep. Instead, he'd spent much of the night tweaking his original plans, working into the wee hours of the morning. He'd come to the realization that what he'd envisioned for the Ninth Ward could still be achieved, and without the stain of gentrification blemishing his project. It just took looking at it in a different way.

The blueprint of the building would stand as is, with a few adjustments to the scope in order to make up for the reduction in the cost of rent. Brazilian cherrywood floors and a waterfall treatment in the lobby would have been nice, but they were not necessities. It was those types of minor tweaks that would make a huge difference in cutting costs.

It was possible that he could still draw in some new people to the area, but that was no longer his main goal. He didn't want to price people out of the neighborhood. He wanted to build a safe, aesthetically pleasing residential and retail building that could serve the people who'd lived in the Ninth Ward all their lives, and who were committed to making the neighborhood the best it could be.

The door opened and a woman dressed in a severe gray suit with curly black hair poked her head out and said, "Mr. Alexander, you may come in."

Upon entering the room, Damien was surprised to discover that it wasn't as enormous as he would have expected. It was only medium-sized, with an eight-seater conference table done in a rich wood much like the door. There was a stately secretary desk in the corner, and another table with a silver coffeepot and tea service.

"Damien," Michael Berger called as he came into the office from a door on the opposite end. "Sorry we couldn't meet in the conference room. It's being used. My office will have to do."

This was his office? Damn, talk about life goals.

"This is fine," Damien said, as if he had meetings in offices the size of Alexander Properties' entire suite everyday.

"Can I get you some coffee? Tea? Water?" Berger asked.

"Thanks. Black, one sugar," Damien answered.

He actually made his own coffee? Nice.

Bringing the coffee to the conference table, he set a mug before Damien and took the seat kitty-corner to his.

"Langley will be in shortly," the other man said.

"Really?" Damien said, nearly choking on the hot coffee he'd just sipped. Langley McGowan, the managing partner, was the only one of the foursome Damien had yet to meet.

"I've been thinking a lot about the project you want

to do south of the industrial canal. In fact, I've had a team researching the area over the past few weeks. I think you may have something here—"

The door opened and Langley McGowan, with his distinguished beard and thick eyebrows, walked in.

Berger made introductions, and within minutes they were all settled and getting down to business.

"We've looked at the plans you sent, and honestly, I'm impressed and a little surprised that no one has thought of it sooner," Berger said. "That area has been ripe for a comeback for years. But, for some reason, it's been forgotten."

"I understand that you're a native of the Ninth Ward," McGowan said.

"Yes," Damien answered. "I grew up there."

Wait? Was that pride he heard in his own voice?

Yes, it was.

Suddenly, Damien felt like a poseur. He hadn't earned the right to take any pride in what the neighborhood had become. He'd purposely stayed away while others put in the hard work to make the Ninth Ward better.

He was going to change that. These past weeks with April had showed him just how much there was left to do, and how much of an impact he could make if he just stepped up and did some good in his old neighborhood.

"We think what you've come up with is great," Berger said. "But after studying the landscape, my team has come up with something bigger and better."

The man pressed a button and two panels on the left wall began to separate. Behind them, a projection screen appeared.

If this was the kind of setup Berger had in his office, Damien was happy he never got the chance to see the conference room. He'd probably choke on his envy.

Berger tapped a couple of keys on the laptop that had been sitting on the table, and a map of the Ninth Ward appeared. The streets that bordered the neighborhood were highlighted yellow and a smaller area was shaded in red.

"This is the location you've proposed for Alexander Quarters," Berger said. "However, after delving deeper, we've discovered that this area would be more advantageous." Another map was superimposed onto the first. "It is more heavily traveled, with easy access to the river and to the Bywater and Faubourg Marigny neighborhoods. We ran a couple of initial numbers with our developer and discovered that erecting a residential and retail center in this area will attract more than twice the amount of foot traffic, especially with the expansion of the Rampart streetcar line."

As Damien studied the map, a sickening feeling settled in his gut.

"That area isn't one hundred percent available," he said. "There are already occupants there. The church, for instance."

And A Fresh Start.

A cagey smile drew across Langley McGowan's face.

"I've have it on good authority that Saint Katherine's will soon merge with another parish. The archdiocese has discussed it for a number of years. They've decided it's the best move for the church."

Dammit. Damien couldn't skirt around the issue any longer.

"There's a community program that uses the building adjacent to the church," Damien said. "I actually volunteer there. Their summer program is vital to the community."

McGowan waved his hand as if it was an annoying fly instead of an essential part of so many kids' lives.

"We'll figure something out when it comes to the community program," he said. "We'll buy them a new building to hold their summer program, if that's necessary."

The offer made Damien feel marginally better, but he also knew it wouldn't be as easy as just relocating A Fresh Start to another facility.

Those kids had worked hard to start up their café and the community garden. Just picking up and moving them somewhere else wouldn't solve the problem. They would have to say goodbye to all the blood, sweat and tears they'd put into that place.

He thought about what April's reaction to this news would be and the sick feeling in his stomach grew.

"Our data people have been running the numbers. Because so many people never returned following Hurricane Katrina, there is an impressive amount of space available."

The enthusiasm in the other man's voice scaled along Damien's nerves like nails down a chalkboard. How could he be excited that so many people hadn't been able to return after being forced out of their homes by Katrina's floodwaters?

Yet, hadn't Damien felt the same way? This entire time, his goal with Alexander Quarters had been, in part, to capitalize on the misfortune of those who'd been run out by Katrina. And, instead of coming up with a solution to help bring them back home, he'd sought to develop something that would keep them out.

Damien felt so slimy that he suddenly felt the need to shower.

"This can turn out to be a very lucrative venture," Langley McGowan said. "Thank you for bringing this area to our attention."

Damien didn't want the man's thanks. He no longer wanted his help, either. He didn't care how lucrative this venture could be. This was no longer about money.

It was amazing how quickly his perspective had changed. If Michael Berger had come to him just a month ago with the ideas he'd just outlined, Damien would have jumped in with both feet. But after witnessing all the hard work that had been poured into the various projects around the Ninth Ward, and seeing the pride with which the residents worked to resurrect the neighborhood from the ashes of Katrina, how could he go along with something like this?

His initial plans only pertained to a small portion of the Ninth Ward. What sat on the screen before him right then encompassed an area at least four times the size of what he'd first envisioned. He could not pretend to be okay with this.

But Damien also understood how these things worked. The McGowan Group didn't need *him* to tell them when, what and how to conduct business. If he told them that he no longer thought it was a good idea to build in the Ninth Ward, they would simply go on without him. They didn't need his permission.

The thought of the McGowan Group bulldozing their way over A Fresh Start was more than Damien could handle.

He had to figure out a way to make this right.

Chapter 11

April stood with her hands on her hips outside the newly installed gate that surrounded the small garden at A Fresh Start.

"What happened?" she asked, disbelief suffusing her voice as she stared at the dozens of plantings that had been dug up and tossed around. Tiny vegetables that had just started to take root had been ripped from the soil, the rows of neatly tilled dirt marred with the deep impressions of footprints.

"Vandals," Simeon said. He pointed to the piece of chain-link fence that was pulled back slightly. "We're thinking they snuck in over there. Based on the size of the opening, they couldn't have been that big. It was probably just some teens who decided to go out and cause trouble."

April let out a rare but well-deserved curse. "The

kids will be devastated when they see this. All that hard work they've put into it, gone, just like that."

"Some of the vegetables were just starting to sprout," Simeon said, gesturing to the small green tomatoes that now lay on the ground instead of hanging on the vine where they should have been.

April shook her head. "I'm going to have to call Jodi at the community gardens to see if they have any they can spare."

"First, we'll call the police," Simeon said.

"We should, although without any cameras I don't know what good it's going to do."

"Maybe someone in the neighborhood saw something. You never know." He clamped a hand on her shoulder. "Look at it this way. The kids will learn one of the biggest life lessons there is, that disappointments can come at a moment's notice."

"Is this your way of looking at the bright side?" she asked him.

He shrugged in that ever-optimistic way of his, managing to wring a laugh from her when all April wanted to do was hit something, preferably the little bastards who'd terrorized their gardens.

Maybe Simeon had the right idea. It was a life lesson, not just for the kids in the program, but for her, too. She knew that setbacks like this one were to be expected. Not every kid in this neighborhood would be saved. Her job was to work with those they'd managed to reach and make sure they didn't fall in with the likes of those who'd caused this mess last night.

April bent down to start clearing away the discarded vegetables, but then decided against it. If the police were coming it was better not to disrupt the crime scene. Instead, she took out her phone so that she could snap a few pictures.

When she looked at the screen, April noticed that she had two missed calls from Damien, along with a text message that read Need to talk to you now.

When she called him back, he picked up on the first ring.

"Hey," she greeted. "You needed something?"

"Yes, where are you?" he asked.

"At A Fresh Start. There was an incident overnight," she said, looking around at the gardens.

"Is everything okay?" Damien asked, concern in his voice.

"Everything except for our gardens," she said. She waved a hand. "I'll tell you about it later. I had a couple of missed calls from you. What did you need?"

"I'll…uh…explain it to you when I get there. Give me about an hour."

April didn't like the hesitancy she heard in his voice. There was something off about it. "Okay," she said. "I'll talk to you then."

To her surprise, the police arrived ten minutes later. April would have thought there would be more pressing issues commanding their attention, but apparently it was a slow crime day in the city. That was something to be thankful for, at least.

However, as she expected, there wasn't all that much the police could do about the vandalism. They took pictures of the shoe impressions in the dirt, and took statements from a couple of the neighboring shop owners. However, they warned April, Simeon and LaDonna, who had arrived just after the police, that the backlog for their detectives was months long, and it wasn't likely that this would be high on the list of priorities.

Before leaving, the police officers, who both revealed that they'd worked in the city's Seventh District for several years, thanked April and the others for the work they were doing with the kids at A Fresh Start.

"I've worked these streets for a long time and I've noticed a difference in the way the kids behave since the start of this program. I can tell which kids attend and those who don't. The kids from A Fresh Start are more respectful and more open to talking to us. You all probably don't hear it enough, but I want to thank you for what you do."

"I second that," the other police officer added.

Emotion clogged April's throat. Apparently, it was the same for her colleagues, as well. No one was able to speak for several moments.

"Thank you so much," April said when she was finally able to find her voice. "We appreciate it."

Once law enforcement left, April and the others headed inside. There was nothing left for them to do right now. As part of their hard life lessons exercise, Simeon suggested that the kids help to clean up the mess from last night's vandalism.

They'd all agreed that it was the right course of action, but it made April even more pissed. The cleanup would eat into their practice time for the streetcar line groundbreaking. Rehearsals were going well; however, the kids still had a long way to go if they were going to perform in front of a live audience. They needed all the practice time they could get.

She'd just turned the corner on her way to her music classroom when she spotted Damien coming through the front door of the center. Just seeing him made some of the tension that had built up in her shoulders float away.

"Hello," she greeted him. Not even bothering to check that there was no one around, she slipped her arms around his waist and stood on tiptoes to brush a kiss over his lips. "I could use a little distraction today after the morning we've had."

"What happened?" Damien asked.

She told him about the vandalism.

"The police came over to take statements, but I know the NOPD has a lot on their plates. They don't have time to worry about a couple of knuckleheads coming in and tearing up our little garden."

"You have it on the books. That's a start. Maybe it'll encourage them to step up patrols here," Damien said.

"Hopefully." April tightened her hold on him. "So, what is it that you needed to speak to me about? My mom is usually the only incessant caller I have to look out for. You had me worried with those two missed calls."

April felt him tense up.

"Damien?" She leaned back so she could look up at him. "What's going on?"

He took her by the hand and they walked back down the hallway to the coffee bar. He brought her to the same table where they'd sat over a month ago when he first came here, asking her to escort him to various events this summer. He took her hand in his, linking them at the center of the table.

"I just came back from a meeting with the McGowan Group."

April's brows rose. "And?"

"And they like my idea," he said.

"Which idea? The one that we talked about? The idea to build a complex with affordable housing for the residents already living here?"

"The discussion didn't get that far," he said. He tipped his head back and let out another annoyed sigh. April's suspicions grew. So did her unease.

"I thought that's what you were going to propose to them?" she asked.

"I never got the chance to propose anything," he said. "As soon as the meeting began, they proposed their own plan." He looked around the room, up at the ceiling, beyond her shoulder. Finally, he brought his eyes back to hers and said, "They want this space."

April pulled her hand out of his hold, as if he'd burned her all of a sudden.

"What exactly does that mean?" she asked.

"They have a plan to develop an area that's over four times the size of my original plan. It would cover several blocks. However, they think this spot would work better than the space I bought up around the Industrial Canal. The proximity to the river and major thoroughfares has more appeal."

"Well, did you tell them they can't have this space?"

Damien held his hands out. "How am I supposed to stop them? How can *anyone* stop them? By the end of the meeting they were already talking about approaching the archdiocese about buying this land. Once a group with that kind of power gets it in their heads to do something, there's no stopping them."

April stared at him across the table. Her blood reached boiling levels. "And you're the one who put it in their heads," she said.

Damien put his hands up. "Don't blame me for this."

"Don't blame you? Who exactly should I blame then, Damien? We were just fine here in the Ninth Ward, slowly rebuilding our community one brick at a time. Then you come in here with your grand ideas on how to 'fix' everything, and now we may lose A Fresh Start? Who do I blame for this?"

"Michael Berger already said that he would be willing to secure a new building for the program."

"We don't want a new building. We are just fine exactly where we are."

"You just got vandalized," Damien said, pointing toward the gardens.

"Don't you dare use what happened last night as an excuse."

"Why shouldn't I?" Damien said. "It's par for the course when it comes to this neighborhood." He ran a palm down his face. "Look, I know this news is unexpected, but it doesn't necessarily have to be a bad thing, April. The McGowan Group can provide the funding you need to turn A Fresh Start into a full-time program. It would be a drop in the bucket for them. Make that one of your demands for having to relocate."

April wasn't ready to buy into his silver-lining scenario just yet.

"You trying to paint this picture in a different light doesn't change the fact that they want to destroy what we've built," she said. "And it also doesn't change the fact that if it wasn't for you, this conglomerate would never have put us on their radar. If we allow this to happen, it can change the entire makeup of this community, Damien."

A thought occurred to her. She looked over at him, and it was as if her eyes were opening for the first time.

"But, then again, that's what you wanted from the start, isn't it?" April accused.

He looked at her, then quickly averted his eyes, but April still caught the guilt that flashed across his face.

"I knew it," she said. She huffed out a humorless laugh. "Despite everything we've talked about over these past few weeks, your goal never changed, did it?"

Just as Damien opened his mouth to spout whatever lame excuse he'd prepared, April's phone rang. She rudely picked it up and answered it, despite being in the middle of a conversation.

"April—" Damien started, but she stopped him, holding a finger up in the universal "give me a minute" gesture.

"This is April Knight," she answered.

It felt as if every drop of blood drained from her face as she listened to the person on the other end of the line. April closed her eyes and cradled her forehead in her palm.

"Please tell me this is a joke," she whispered.

"April, what is it?" Damien asked, the concern in his voice coming across clearly.

Ignoring his question, April rose from the table.

"I'll be right there," she said to the person on the other end of the line. She disconnected the call and looked over at Damien. "I have to go and take care of something."

"What is it?" He stood. "Do you need my help?"

"No," she said. "You've helped enough."

Damien stood there in the café at A Fresh Start, debating whether he should follow April. But when the alert went off on his phone—his reminder about his lunch with Kurt—he decided against it. If the past ten minutes were any indication of how things would go, April would have probably run him over with her car the minute she saw him.

Instead, Damien drove out to Mid-City, pulling into Kurt's driveway fifteen minutes after leaving A Fresh Start. He sat behind the wheel, contemplating calling Kurt and rescheduling their weekly lunch. With the mood he was in, he wouldn't be good company for anybody.

His cell phone rang and Kurt's number flashed on the screen.

Damien pressed the Bluetooth button on his console. "I'm right outside," he said by way of greeting.

"I know that," Kurt answered. "I was calling to ask if you planned to come inside. I've got fried shrimp. They'll get cold and rubbery if they sit for too long."

"Yeah, I'll be inside in a minute," Damien said.

He gripped the steering wheel, unable to get the picture of April's face when he told her about the McGowan Group's plans out of his mind. But what really got to him was when she accused him of wanting this all along.

He had, hadn't he?

He was getting exactly what he wanted. The investors he'd sought were willing to make his dream a reality.

So why in the hell did it feel as if he had lead sitting in his stomach, weighing him down like a rusty anchor?

Damien got out of the car and trudged up the ramp leading to the porch. As he approached, the front door opened and Kurt appeared. He maneuvered his chair so that Damien could come in, and then led the way into the kitchen. Damien could smell the unique aroma of shrimps fried in cornmeal and spices, just like his mom used to make.

There was a salad bowl filled with leafy greens. A small plate with tomato slices and pickles sat next to it. A long loaf of French bread from the Leidenheimer Baking Company—a New Orleans staple for making po'boys—sat on the counter next to the other fixings.

"I've got canned drinks in the fridge," Kurt said as he rolled over to the cabinet and used the elevation button on his chair to lift him up high enough to retrieve two plates from the cabinet. Damien didn't make a move to help him.

As Kurt fixed their sandwiches, he regaled Damien with the latest story about his hippie neighbors who were constantly being arrested for indecent exposure. This time the couple decided to work in their flower-beds in the buff, in the middle of the day.

Damien usually found their antics entertaining, but he just wasn't feeling it today.

"What's up with you?" Kurt asked when Damien responded to his story with a halfhearted chuckle.

"Nothing," he answered. "Just a lot on my mind today."

Damien put his elbows up on the table and folded his hands over his sandwich. He bowed his head as his brother prayed over their lunch, but he couldn't bring himself to take a bite. He watched as Kurt started in on his sandwich.

After several moments passed, Damien asked, "How is it that you're not still filled with rage?"

His brother stopped midbite. "Filled with rage about what?"

"About what happened to you. About the fact that you're stuck in this chair for the rest of your life because some bastard shot you down in the street?"

Kurt's head snapped back in surprise. "Where is this coming from?"

"I just never understood how you got past the anger so quickly."

"What good would being filled with rage do? You read some new study that says that anger helps paraplegics walk again?" Kurt drawled.

Damien ignored his mocking tone. "I know the rage doesn't help anything, but damn, Kurt! I'm more upset over it than you are. I still can't go into that neighborhood without remembering what happened to you and to dad. I swear, it makes me so damn angry I can hardly see straight.

"That's why this thing with April is so hard." Damien ran a palm down his face. "She's all about saving the Ninth Ward, but how in the hell can I work to save a neighborhood that did this to you?"

Kurt placed his sandwich on his plate, and with deliberate slowness, wiped at the corners of his mouth.

"Is that what you think?" his brother asked. "You think the *neighborhood* did this to me?"

"How else should I see it? You were just minding your own business and someone shot you down. The bastard probably still lives there, walking along those same streets without a care in the world."

"He doesn't live there anymore," Kurt said.

"How do you know? The police never caught him."

"And they never will, because he's dead."

"What are you talking about?" Damien asked. "The police were never even able to identify the suspect. How do you know that he's dead?"

"I knew who shot me," his brother answered. "He was shot and killed himself just a few weeks after I was shot."

Damien shook his head, as if that would clear the confusion caused by his brother's words. "Kurt, what in the hell are you talking about? You were just walking down the street and you were shot in the back."

"I was selling drugs," Kurt said.

Damien could do nothing but sit there as a wave of shock crashed into him.

He jumped out of his chair and paced to the other end of the kitchen, trying to physically distance himself from the lie his brother had just told. Because it *was* a lie. It *had* to be a lie.

"You were not selling drugs," Damien argued. "Why would you even say that?"

"Because, I was," Kurt answered. "The person who shot me had come to buy drugs, but he didn't have the money. He tried to steal them from me. I was shot in the back because I turned to run away from him."

Damien collapsed into his seat again. It felt as if the world had just slipped out from underneath him. His older brother? The person he'd looked up to for all these years? A drug dealer?

"How? You…" He couldn't bring himself to say the words out loud.

"I made stupid choices," Kurt said. "I did that, and I paid for them. You want to know why I'm not angry? It's because I realize that I'm lucky to be in this chair. I'm lucky to be alive, Damien. I could have died that day. *I* put myself in that situation. Don't put the blame on the Ninth Ward. The only one who deserves blame for what happened to me is me."

Kurt backed his chair away from the table and came over to sit right in front of Damien. Kurt clamped his hands over Damien's shoulders and gave them a firm squeeze.

As he looked up at his brother, Damien felt as if his entire being had been caught up in a tornado of confusion.

"Look, Damien, you explained what you wanted to do with that land you bought, and I supported you because you're my brother and I'll always support you. But I don't believe in it.

"There's a lot of good already going on in the old neighborhood. It's had a bad rap for a long time, but people like April are trying to change it. She and the rest of those folks at that youth center are seeing to it that the kids who live there now won't make the same choices I made." Kurt tapped him in the center of his chest. "They need to see people like *you*. Those who made it out the right way. If you really want to leave a legacy in the world, help those kids make something of themselves. Help give them a neighborhood they can be proud of."

And just like that, Damien knew what he needed to do.

Chapter 12

April entered the NOPD's seventh precinct on Dwyer Road, her heart beating as wildly as it had when she first received the call from the arresting officer. She walked up to the service counter.

"I'm here to see Officer Pickney," she said in a breathless voice.

"Are you April Knight?" came a voice just beyond her shoulder.

April turned to find a middle-aged officer with a full beard and a gleaming bald head.

"I am," she answered. She reached her hand out to shake his hand. "Are you Officer Pickney?"

He nodded.

"Thank you so much for calling me," she said.

"Thank you for coming." He gestured for her to follow him. "They're in here."

April followed him into a small room. Linsey and

another girl, one April had seen around the neighborhood but whom she'd never met, sat at a plain wooden table. April wasn't sure she could feel any more dismayed after her argument with Damien, but she'd been wrong. Disappointment pummeled her as she looked down on Linsey's bent head.

"They were caught stuffing various items down their shirts. The convenience store has them on surveillance tape. When we asked her who we could call, she gave us your name and number."

April nodded. "Have they been charged?"

"The owner of the store is still in with another of the deputies. He hasn't decided yet if he's going to bring charges."

"Linsey," April called, but the girl refused to look at her. "So, you had me come all the way over here, but you're not going to speak to me?" April asked her.

"I didn't want my mom here," the girl finally murmured, her eyes still focused on the table.

"And who is this?" April asked, gesturing to the other girl who'd also decided that being mute was the way to go.

"Erica," Linsey said.

Finally, Linsey looked up at her. Her bottom lip trembled.

"You know what will happen to you if the owner of that store decides to press charges, don't you?" April asked.

She nodded, and then burst out crying.

As Linsey's shoulders shook with her sobs, April wanted to feel sorry for her, but that wall of disappointment and anger still blocked all other emotions. Between the vandalism, Damien's betrayal and now

Linsey's arrest, it was just too much for one day. It felt as if everything she'd worked for over these past two years meant nothing. Had she made one bit of difference?

When she'd first started at A Fresh Start, April knew it would be impossible to prevent every kid from going down the wrong path. But she thought she was on the right track with Linsey. She'd seen something in the young teen, and had worked so hard to cultivate it, hoping the music would be her saving grace in the same way it had saved April.

Yet, look where they were. Linsey sure as hell couldn't practice the cello in jail.

"We're going to have to call your mother," April said.

"I know," Linsey replied in a small voice. She hiccupped and wiped her nose with the back of her hand.

Such a childlike gesture.

She *was* a child. But she would learn a very adult lesson today. Linsey would have to learn that actions had consequences.

April released a tired breath. She was suddenly exhausted.

"I'll go get Officer Pickney. He'll need to call both of your parents."

She turned for the door, but was stopped by Linsey's soft-spoken voice.

"Ms. April?" the girl called.

April turned around.

"I'm sorry."

Emotion welled up in her throat, making it hard to swallow. April knew speaking was out of the question. Instead, she nodded and left the room.

She found Officer Pickney at the coffee station, adding an enormous amount of sugar to a small foam cup. He spotted her and gestured his cup toward the room.

"The store owner decided not to press charges," the officer said.

The tension that had built up in April's shoulders released in a wave of relief. "Thank goodness," she said. "I don't know the other girl, but Linsey is a good kid."

The officer shrugged. "I could tell. She didn't mouth off like some of them do. Probably just got caught up in the moment. You know how kids are."

"You're being very understanding. I appreciate that."

"The store owner wants to speak to you. He needed to get back to work, but said he'd like to talk about maybe partnering with the youth center. Said maybe if he gives the kids jobs, they wouldn't turn to stealing." Officer Pickney smiled. "I've known Mr. Johnson for a long time. Before, he would have had those girls face a judge. I'd say what you all are doing over at A Fresh Start is having an impact on attitudes throughout the entire community." He winked. "Good job."

The knot returned to April's throat. She managed to give him a small smile, but as she left the police precinct she still couldn't shake the awful feeling that hit her the moment she saw Linsey sitting at that scarred wooden table.

She got into her car and gripped the wheel, but she didn't start it. Instead, she looked out at the police cars lining the street outside the building, imagining other kids from A Fresh Start in the backseat. Did she have what it took to prevent that? Or was she wasting her time?

Just as April reached to start the ignition, her phone rang. It was her agent, Carlos.

There was an uptick in her heartbeat as she stared at the phone. Carlos usually texted her. He only called when he wanted to hear her reaction.

"Hello?" April finally answered.

She listened to Carlos's excited voice on the other end of the line. She was certain that he was disappointed in her reaction. Instead of a scream of delight, April groaned at the news Carlos had just imparted.

Just like that, life had thrown her another curveball. And she had no idea what she was going to do with it.

April pulled into a parking spot less than a block away from her house. As she trudged along the sidewalk, it felt as if her legs were filled with lead. The weight of everything that had transpired over the course of today was just too much to handle.

On top of the vandalism, Damien's revelation about what the McGowan Group wanted to do to the youth center and Linsey's arrests, April found out on her return to A Fresh Start that Nicole had just accepted a new job in Tampa, and would be leaving at the end of the month. It made the decision April faced even harder.

Her steps faltered when she came upon her house.

Damien sat on the steps leading up to her porch, his knees braced apart, his elbows resting on his thighs. He clutched his hands together as if in prayer.

When he noticed her, he remained silent, his eyes tracking her steps.

April walked up to him and took a seat beside him on the porch steps. They both looked straight ahead, not saying anything for several minutes.

"How's it going?" Damien finally asked.

"I've had better days," she answered.

She spent the next ten minutes explaining the situation with Linsey. It was the phone call from the police precinct that had cut their conversation short this morning.

"I don't know why I'm even doing this, Damien. I thought I was making a difference, but I don't know anymore."

"How can you say that?" he asked. "I've seen you with those kids, April. More important, I've seen how the kids are when they're with you. You make them want to be better people, the same way you did with me."

She looked over at him, wanting to believe him.

"Don't give up on them," Damien said. "You *are* making a difference."

"But is it enough? I don't know if I'm really cut out for this. Maybe I *should* just go back to touring. That's what I'm good at."

"Where is this coming from, April?"

April covered her face with both palms. "My agent called this afternoon. I've been granted an audition with the Boston Pops."

She heard Damien release a low whistle. "Wow," he said. "That's the one, isn't it? The one you've wanted."

"Ever since I was ten years old," she said.

"You have to do it."

She spread her fingers wide enough to peer at him.

"You have to," Damien said again. "This is your dream."

"But what about A Fresh Start? How can I just bail on them?"

"You're not bailing on them, and you're definitely not going to bail on Linsey." Damien captured her wrists and gently tugged her hands from her face. "You can make this work. Even if you have to teach your music class via the web. We're going to figure out a way for you to do both, April. Call your agent and accept that audition."

"Does it even matter?" she asked. "If the McGowan Group is going to come in and bulldoze over A Fresh Start, what does it matter?"

"They won't," Damien said. "Well, the building may not stand, but A Fresh Start will."

April's heart started to pound with anticipation. "What do you mean by that?"

"After I left you this morning, I went over to Kurt's and he chewed my ass out."

"As all big brothers have the right to do," April interjected.

"I don't know if I agree with that," Damien said. "But, this time, he was right. He gave me a lot to think about. When I left Kurt's, I went back to see Michael Berger and I laid down a set of conditions.

"The McGowan Group and Alexander Properties are now in a formal partnership to develop both upscale and affordable housing in the Ninth Ward. The land that I purchased is going to be the home to A Fresh Start's new state-of-the-art facility."

April's hands flew to her mouth in shock. "What?"

"The McGowan Group has agreed to build you all a new facility. You can forget about that grant you all are trying to get, as well. They're signing on as A Fresh Start's official corporate sponsor. You'll have the funds you need to turn it into a year-round program, and hire more staff so that you can offer a wider range of activities for the kids."

"Oh, my God," April breathed. "How did you do this?"

"I appealed to their more charitable side," Damien said. "I also explained that the residents of the Ninth Ward would probably be more welcoming if the McGowan Group showed that they are willing to work with them and not against them. They agreed."

April was so filled with emotion she could barely speak.

Damien turned to her. Once again, he took her hands away from her face, this time encapsulating them between his own.

"You opened my eyes to things I refused to see for so long, April. Because of you, I see our old neighborhood for what it is now, not for what it used to be." He pressed a kiss to her fingers. "But, more important, because of you, I now see how much brighter my future will be if I get to share it with the woman I love.

"I love you, April. It took me a while to see it, but I *do* see it now. I see how good we are together. I never want to be without you again."

"What if I go to Boston?"

"That's what airplanes and four-day workweeks are for," Damien said with a grin. "We'll make it work. We have to, because I refuse to go back to what we were a month ago."

He caressed her jaw. "I love you. I've always loved you as a friend, but you're so much more than that, April. You're the woman I want to spend the rest of my life with."

Her eyes fell shut as a wave of longing and contentment washed over her.

"I've wanted that for so long," April finally admitted. She opened her eyes. "Does this really happen? Do people really get to live out their fairy tale? Can I truly have you, A Fresh Start and the Boston Pops?"

Damien leaned in close and brushed his lips against hers.

"You deserve to have it all," he said. "And if you'll let me, I want to be the one who gives it to you."

Epilogue

Damien settled into the first seat of the rearmost row of Boston Symphony Hall. He'd changed seats three times in the past five minutes and was itching to spring up again. As much as he tried, he couldn't stop his leg's incessant bouncing. April had just been called up for her audition. Damien was pretty sure he would throw up from the nerves swirling in his stomach before she played a single note.

She walked onto the stage with more confidence than Damien had ever seen in anyone. Ever.

She had this. When it came to her music, nothing could stop her.

As she started her audition—a piece she'd written specifically for this tryout—April's passion for her music shone through. Damien closed his eyes and allowed her magnificent performance to take him away.

When she finished, there were no applause from the judges, although it had been that way with the previous musicians, so Damien didn't bother to take offense. He kept his jubilation in check, but on the inside he was cheering her on like a madman.

He couldn't be any prouder of her.

And he couldn't be any more in love with her.

When he'd walked into A Fresh Start at the beginning of the summer, Damien had never imagined how different his life would be three months later. Not only had he rediscovered his love for his old neighborhood, but he'd found a love he never knew he could have with April.

He'd already accepted that she would earn a spot in the Boston Symphony Orchestra. After that performance, how could they *not* accept her? But as he told April several months ago, they were going to make this work.

Sometimes the fairy tale did come true. They could both have it all.

Damien stood as April walked up the darkened aisle. She quickened her steps as she neared him and wrapped her arms around him in a hug that nearly took him down.

"You were amazing," Damien said.

"It felt amazing," April answered. The huge smile stretching across her face was the most beautiful thing Damien had ever seen. This was what pure happiness looked like.

"As far as this audition goes, I don't think you have anything to worry about," he said. "It's in the bag."

"It doesn't matter." April shook her head. "I won't take it even if they offer the position," she said.

He pulled back. "What?"

"My dream was to audition. I did that. That's good enough for me." She kissed his chin. "I have what I want back home in New Orleans. You and the kids at A Fresh Start. You're all I need."

* * * * *

REQUEST YOUR FREE BOOKS!

2 FREE NOVELS
PLUS 2 FREE GIFTS!

KIMANI ROMANCE ™

Love's ultimate destination!

YES! Please send me 2 FREE Harlequin® Kimani™ Romance novels and my 2 FREE gifts (gifts are worth about $10). After receiving them, if I don't wish to receive any more books, I can return the shipping statement marked "cancel." If I don't cancel, I will receive 4 brand-new novels every month and be billed just $5.44 per book in the U.S. or $5.99 per book in Canada. That's a savings of at least 16% off the cover price. It's quite a bargain! Shipping and handling is just 50¢ per book in the U.S. and 75¢ per book in Canada.* I understand that accepting the 2 free books and gifts places me under no obligation to buy anything. I can always return a shipment and cancel at any time. Even if I never buy another book, the two free books and gifts are mine to keep forever.

168/368 XDN GH4P

Name	(PLEASE PRINT)	
Address		Apt. #
City	State/Prov.	Zip/Postal Code

Signature (if under 18, a parent or guardian must sign)

Mail to the **Reader Service:**
IN U.S.A.: P.O. Box 1867, Buffalo, NY 14240-1867
IN CANADA: P.O. Box 609, Fort Erie, Ontario L2A 5X3

Want to try two free books from another line?
Call 1-800-873-8635 or visit www.ReaderService.com.

* Terms and prices subject to change without notice. Prices do not include applicable taxes. Sales tax applicable in N.Y. Canadian residents will be charged applicable taxes. Offer not valid in Quebec. This offer is limited to one order per household. Not valid for current subscribers to Harlequin® Kimani™ Romance books. All orders subject to credit approval. Credit or debit balances in a customer's account(s) may be offset by any other outstanding balance owed by or to the customer. Please allow 4 to 6 weeks for delivery. Offer available while quantities last.

Your Privacy—The Reader Service is committed to protecting your privacy. Our Privacy Policy is available online at www.ReaderService.com or upon request from the Reader Service.

We make a portion of our mailing list available to reputable third parties that offer products we believe may interest you. If you prefer that we not exchange your name with third parties, or if you wish to clarify or modify your communication preferences, please visit us at www.ReaderService.com/consumerschoice or write to us at Reader Service Preference Service, P.O. Box 9062, Buffalo, NY 14240-9062. Include your complete name and address.

KROM15

THE WORLD IS BETTER WITH

Romance

Harlequin has everything from contemporary, passionate and heartwarming to suspenseful and inspirational stories.

Whatever your mood, we have a romance just for you!

Connect with us to find your next great read, special offers and more.

f /HarlequinBooks

🐦 @HarlequinBooks

www.HarlequinBlog.com

www.Harlequin.com/Newsletters

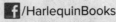

H HARLEQUIN®

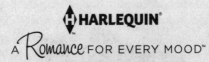

A *Romance* FOR EVERY MOOD™

www.Harlequin.com

"I understand whenever a Steele sees a woman he wants, he goes after her. It appears Tyson's targeted you, Hunter," Mo said as she leaned over. "Maybe he thinks there's unfinished business between the two of you."

It took less than a minute for Tyson to reach their table. He glanced around and smiled at everyone. "Evening, ladies." And then his gaze returned to hers and he said, "Hello, Hunter. It's been a while."

Hunter inhaled deeply, surprised that he had remembered her after all. But what really captured her attention were his features. He was still sinfully handsome, with skin the color of creamy chocolate and a mouth that was shaped too darn beautifully to belong to any man. And his voice was richer and a lot deeper than she'd remembered.

HKMREXP0216R

Before she could respond to what he'd said, Mo and Kat thanked him for the drinks as they stood. Hunter looked at them. "Where are you two going?" she asked.

"Kat and I thought we'd move closer to that big-screen television to catch the last part of the basketball game. I think my team is winning."

As soon as they grabbed their drinks off the table and walked away, Tyson didn't waste time claiming one of the vacated seats. Hunter glanced over and met his gaze while thinking that the only thing worse than being deserted was being deserted and left with a Steele.

She took a sip of her drink and then said, "I want to thank you for my drink, as well. That was nice of you."

"I'm a nice person."

The jury is still out on that, she thought. "I'm surprised you remember me, Tyson."

He chuckled, and the sound was so stimulating it seemed to graze her skin. "Trust me. I remember you. And do you know what I remember most of all?"

"No, what?"

He leaned over the table as if to make sure his next words were for her ears only. "The fact that we never slept together."

Don't miss
POSSESSED BY PASSION
by Brenda Jackson,
available March 2016 wherever
Harlequin® Kimani Romance™
books and ebooks are sold!